Perfect 10

By Twisha Rao

One

"5, 6, 7-"

"Sorry I'm late!" I cried as I ran into the acrobatic dancing studio in the Atlantic City Statewide School of Dance, which was a prestigious dance school that had dance classes for almost every style of dance one could imagine. I started dancing when I was 12 years old and I was pretty good, but I wouldn't say *amazing*. I would've stayed in my old dance school, but as soon as I heard that there were a couple openings in this school, there was no way I could refuse. I actually had to audition along with hundreds of other students in order to get into this school, and surprisingly, I was one of the students who'd made the cut.

"Krithi Sridhar, you're 15 minutes late! You know that's unacceptable," screamed Mrs. Félicité, who had knocked me out of my thoughts and jerked me back to reality with those words. I looked at her apologetically as the class jeered at me. I immediately turned red in embarrassment and looked away.

"Well, why were you late?" Mrs. Félicité demanded.

"I'm sorry. I was busy. I have back- to- back classes," I said. Mrs. Félicité was a very strict and straightforward teacher. She always pointed out any mistakes and always set high standards for her students, such as *never be late*, or *always stick a landing*. We all knew that the latter was next to impossible, but none of us ever had the courage to actually tell our teacher that. She was tall, slender, and almost all the time, she wore an extremely heavy layer of makeup on her face, which always consisted of a blend of turquoise and cobalt blue eyeshadow (her two favorite colors), black eyeliner, some mascara, very heavy blush, and many layers of lipstick/lip gloss. Sometimes she'd even double her layers. Talk about being a makeup addict!

"Krithi, that's no excuse. Make adjustments to your other class! Acrobatics is way more important. If you don't make any adjustments and come to class late, I'll personally make sure you're kicked out of this dance school."

"Okay, I'll find a way to make it work," I muttered. I knew it was next to impossible if I wanted to "make it work". My art teacher was not as strict as Mrs. Félicité... but she was strict. If I were to compare the two and to decide which one I was going to put first... I'd definitely go with Mrs. Félicité. After that threat, there's no way I'm taking chances.

"You'd better. Now, warm up and I expect to see a perfect acrobatics routine from you and your partner. Don't forget, our state competition is coming up soon."

"How many days?" I asked.

"Don't you dare interrupt me!" Mrs. Félicité snapped.

"Please tell me. I'm trying to figure out if I'm available that day," I said, stretching. "And I didn't mean to interrupt you," I added after she glared at me.

"No! Finish your warm up!"

"Okay... okay." I finished it and I stared at her, waiting for my next instruction.

"Now, show me those acrobatics routines," she instructed next.

"Fine," I said. My partner and I showed her the three routines we needed to perform. As soon as we were done, I looked at her for approval.

"*Not bad*," Mrs. Félicité told me. "But we're striving for greatness." Really? I do an almost perfect routine and all I get is "not bad"? I decided to ignore that, since the last thing I want to do is let Mrs. Félicité take pride in underpraising my routine... not that I cared if anyone else did, but we are talking about the best acrobatic dancing coach in the entire US. Of course, I'd want to impress her. After another hour of what Mrs. Félicité calls "acrobatics practice", class was finally over. Thank goodness for that! I glanced out the window of the gymnasium and caught a glimpse of my brother, Rajesh, and my father sitting in the lobby. Rajesh stared at me, his anxious eyes glued to mine. He knows how strict Mrs. Félicite is. I've told him everything.

Rajesh is my twin brother and a great friend, and the only person I ever hang out with, which was the case since we moved here, and I am so grateful to have him as my brother. Rajesh and I were both born in Amaravati, a city in the state of Andhra Pradesh, which is in India. When I was 7, my parents had a rough relationship, so my mother left us both. Rajesh never knew, but I strongly believed our mother left because he was diagnosed with an anxiety disorder a short while before, but that wasn't his fault, not at all. I've had a diagnosis before, too. I've had depression, but I don't have it anymore. I couldn't imagine which one was worse, anxiety or depression. Both are definitely hard to deal with.

"Hi," Rajesh said after I left the gymnasium and met him in the opulent lobby. "How was it?"

"It was awful," I answered.

"Your routine looked nice... I saw you practicing with your partner."

"Not in my teacher's eyes," I muttered quietly. "Not that I care," I added quickly when I saw Rajesh look at me with a concerned expression.

"Did Mrs. Félicité fall over 'cause you were late?" Dad teased. We all hated that teacher equivalently, including my father who doesn't hate anyone. It was the first time in years that Dad had made a joke, and I was happy that he was returning to himself, but at the same time, it was kind of annoying.

"Ugh," I said. "Yes, she did freak out... a little. Not much," I added, when I saw Mrs. Félicité's glare out the window of the gymnasium. It was as if her face had the words "GET OUT" written all over it. I lowered my voice to a whisper. "She did scream at me though, about the fact that I have to put acrobatics first and make adjustments to my art class, or else she's going to personally make sure I get kicked out of this school."

"Wow," Rajesh said.

"Yeah." I glanced at the window to make sure Mrs. Félicité wasn't listening, since the window was open. She seemed very busy, organizing her collection of music DVDs for the competition.

"Um... is it just me or is your teacher really angry today?" Rajesh asked.

"Look through the window," I replied. Both of us stared at Mrs. Félicité, who yelled at someone on the phone.

"Does that answer your question?" I asked, as she continued screaming loudly.

"Yes, she's definitely angry."

"When is she not?"

"Why don't we head home. You've had a long day," Dad suggested, breaking our conversation. I could sense a little worry in his tone and I raised my eyebrows at him. "I just need to speak to Mrs. Félicité quickly, and then we will go." He walked into the gymnasium and began to speak to her. Rajesh and I looked at each other.

"Have any idea what that's about?" I asked.

"No idea," Rajesh replied. We stared at them. Dad was talking calmly and Mrs. Félicité looked as if she was about to explode.

"Please," Dad seemed to be saying. "Calm down."

"I WILL NOT CALM DOWN!! HOW COULD KRITHI NOT TELL ME?!" Mrs. Félicité yelled. I blinked in shock. Tell her *what*?!

"It's because she doesn't know yet!" Dad explained, looking even more worried.

"Looks like she's finding out now!" Mrs. Félicité stormed out of the gymnasium.

"Wait, don't tell her! I'd rather do it myself!!" Dad said quickly, but it was too late. Mrs. Félicité already made her way over to me.
"I CAN'T BELIEVE YOU'RE MOVING AWAY BEFORE THE COMPETITION!"

Two

"Dad, what's she talking about?" I asked.

"Um... we are moving... in two days... to Santa Monica," he said quietly. As soon as he finished his sentence, Mrs. Félicité glared at us and stalked back to the gymnasium.

"That's in California! And two days?! What about the acrobatics competition?" I said.

"I'm sorry, but you'll have to miss it," Dad said. I understood a little, so I nodded, but I still felt a little angry that he was putting all of this on us *now*. "Let's go home and continue this there, okay?"

"Fine." As soon as we reached home, Dad had us pack our bags, but Rajesh and I weren't doing anything without answers.

"How could you not tell us that?!" I asked.

"I'm sorry, I had no idea how to tell you-" Dad began, but I stopped him mid sentence with a sharp glare.

"This is all because of Christina right?" Rajesh snapped.

"Who's Christina?" I asked as I stopped glaring.

"She's Dad's *girlfriend*. Remember that business trip he went on to Santa Monica about a month ago? They met there and then became all... okay, let's just say Dad or Christina... whoever it was, fell in love and told the other one. Since his business trip was for a month, they had a great amount of time for dating. Now we're moving because of her, am I correct?!" Dad didn't answer that. Instead, he said,

"Okay, okay. Calm down! I'm sorry I didn't tell you."

"Yeah, whatever," Rajesh muttered.

"Wait a minute. How did you find out, Rajesh?" Dad inquired.

"And why didn't you tell me?" I added. Rajesh looked at us for two seconds.

"I overheard you on a call with her. *You kissed each other goodbye.* I instantly made the connection," he replied simply. "And Krithi, I'm sorry I didn't tell you. It's because I was still processing the information myself. That call happened a few days ago." Dad's cheeks turned red. I decided to ask my question now.

"So is it because of Christina?" I asked.

"No. We are moving because of my job." Dad was always honest to us, no matter what.

"Likely," Rajesh rolled his eyes. He clearly didn't think Dad was being honest this time. Dad seriously looked as if he wanted to scold Rajesh, but he held off because he understood our perspective.

"Let's go pack up. We are leaving in two days," I said, breaking up the tension. This was how it's been ever since our mother left us and we moved away. Rajesh loses his temper easily, Dad argues with Rajesh and then... well... I'm the one solving the arguments.

"Yes, your sister is right," Dad said, looking at me gratefully. I didn't return his smile, Rajesh rolled his eyes and we both went to our bedroom and began packing what we could.

"I don't *want* a new mother," Rajesh eventually admitted.

"It's not like we're going to be getting one anytime soon. Dad's still dating Christina," I assured him, folding clothes and placing them carefully in my suitcase.

"I know, but what if they end up getting *engaged*?" Oh gosh, the thought of my father getting remarried made me more worried than ever. I stayed quiet for a few seconds as I continued folding clothes as I kept thinking about it.

"Don't worry," I eventually told Rajesh, trying to get rid of the thought.

"Probably not, but to be quite honest, I don't like the thought of Dad having a girlfriend either."

"Who knows... maybe she's not that bad," Rajesh said, calming down a bit.

"I guess."

"Time for dinner," Dad called, breaking our conversation. The smell of Indian food wafted from the kitchen. Rajesh and I walked downstairs and sat down at the dining table.

"So, you're all packed?" Dad asked, serving himself food.

"Yup," I said.

"Good. I'm sorry this was all last minute-"

"It's fine," Rajesh immediately interrupted.

"I made your favorite sweet," Dad said, changing the subject.

"You made Gulab Jamun?" Dad almost never makes it.

"Yeah! It's waiting for you, so eat quickly." We finished eating and took our bowls, which each had one of the fried spherical sweets inside a sugary rose syrup. We finished and immediately went back to finish packing.

The two days had gone by quicker than I'd realized, and next thing we knew, we were driving to the airport. We had our first layover in Santa Fe, New Mexico, and then from there, we had a flight to Los Angeles, and after we had landed there, Christina would drive us to her house Santa Monica, which was about a half hour away from the airport. As soon as we landed in New Mexico, we had to get to the gate, because we had a total of 20 minutes before our next flight. Thankfully, we made it through security and to the gate, with 5 minutes left. We boarded the plane to Los Angeles successfully. We were still on land for… who knows how long. So much for hurrying! My thoughts were interrupted when the pilot finally announced the take-off. Seconds later, we were in the sky, and I drifted off to sleep, not thinking about anything.

"Krithi wake up!" Dad called. I woke up and stared at him in confusion.
"We've landed," Rajesh informed me.
"Oh, okay. Thanks," I said, realizing I slept the full duration of the flight. I wasn't exactly the most energetic after waking up, so when I got up from my seat, I had almost accidentally slammed my suitcase to the ground by its wheels. Soon, everyone was staring at us, so we left the plane quickly as soon as we could. We made it out of the plane (thankfully) and saw a woman. At our gate. Smiling the widest smile I've

ever seen. She had long, brown hair, pink lipstick and was slender just like Mrs. Félicité.

"Hello, Anil!"

"Hi, Christina," Dad greeted the woman. They hugged each other.

"Oh, you must be Anil's kids!" Christina realized. She hugged us both tightly. I felt as if I was about to explode if she hugged me for three more seconds.

"Um... yeah. Let go of us, please," I muttered quietly. She smiled and released us.

"What are your names?"

"Krithi," I said.

"Rajesh," said Rajesh.

"Okay! Nice to meet you! It's been far too long." We left, and Christina drove us to her house. Dad and Christina were busy talking, and I was glad of it. That way, Christina wouldn't start talking to us, because there was no way I was having a full on conversation with someone who I'd just met. That scares me... a lot. As soon as the car ride was over, she opened the door to let us inside the house.

"Oh my gosh," I gasped as I stepped into Christina's elegant mansion. There were outdoor pools and lush gardens filled with pretty flowers and waterfalls. There were even palm trees around the pool, making it feel extra tropical. The interior consisted of many, many rooms, luxurious staircases and even a gymnasium.

"I had the gymnasium installed for you, Krithi. Your father told me you loved acrobatics," Christina told me. I smiled and said,

"Thank you."

"I've got our personal chefs making a full course buffet that will last for *days*."

"Oh wow," I said as I stared at the Italian meal set on the table. This was obviously way too much. I didn't say a thing, though, as we sat down and ate whatever we could. Then, we explored the house more.

"This is your bedroom, Krithi," Christina said, showing me to a room on the second floor of the multiple story mansion. I opened the door and gasped. My room had a queen bed, three chintz armchairs and a tabletop waterfall sitting on a white desk. I also had a huge closet that had amazing clothes in every style, though I was curious as to how she knew my size. After thinking about it for a couple seconds, I realized that Dad must've told her, and from the looks of it, she went on a huge shopping spree.

"I have something to take care of," Christina said. "Why don't you unpack? I'll let Rajesh know to unpack as well." She left and I sat down on the bed. A few minutes later, someone knocked on my door. Rajesh came inside. I glanced up and didn't say anything. His smiling expression turned into a concerned one. He sat down next to me.

"What happened?"

"Nothing," I replied, even though that was a total lie. I wished he had bought it, because the last thing I want to do right now is talk about my current feelings. He didn't buy it though, much to my disadvantage.

"Okay, I'm your twin brother. We've known each other our whole lives. I can tell whenever something is bothering you. In this case, lying is pointless," Rajesh informed me. He put a reassuring hand on my shoulder. "You can tell me. I won't tell anyone."

"Okay. I'm just not used to this place," I admitted, looking around the interior of the room.

"I know. I'm not used to it either. I seriously miss our old hometown."

"India or New Jersey?"

"Would it surprise you if I said I missed India more?" I looked at him for a couple seconds and eventually said,

"It doesn't surprise me."

"I do miss New Jersey as well," Rajesh added.

"I miss both places too. Christina is nice and all, but I just don't want her to be Dad's girlfriend." I sighed. "The truth is, I'm scared that Christina is going to do what Mom did to us." The word "Mom" brought terrible memories of the day she left us. I feared that Rajesh wouldn't understand, but he did, because after a few seconds, he said,

"I had that same fear."

"Really?" I asked.

"Yes, although, after thinking about it for a few minutes, I realized that Christina won't do what Mom did to us. Mom didn't want to be with Dad anymore. That's why she left. Christina seems to be obsessed with Dad, judging the fact that she annoyingly compliments him every five minutes, so it doesn't seem like anything would happen too soon." I flinched at the fact that Rajesh still didn't know the real reason Mom left. I buried my face in my hands.

"Are you okay?" Rajesh asked, quickly noticing.

"Yeah," I said, immediately releasing my hands from my face. "Just lost in thought."

"Okay, then. Anyways, the point is, we'll be okay." He wrapped his arm around my shoulders and we just sat there in complete silence, until my phone rang.

"Hello, Krithi." It was Mrs. Félicté.

"Hi," I said. "Why are you calling me? And how do you have my number?" I tried to be as nice as possible, but I found it very strange that she had my number, and Rajesh must've felt the same, because he looked way more anxious than usual. His eyes practically reflected the words: "End the call".

"Oh, your father gave it to me when he told me that you were moving." As soon as those words were said, I breathed a huge sigh of relief. "Good news. You can compete with us in Nationals, as long as you fly over to Dallas, which is where it takes place. You don't necessarily have to be in New Jersey to be on our team... unless you join a new one," she continued, but I didn't hear the last part, because I was too focused on the fact that she said "Nationals". How did her team make it to Nationals? We hadn't done our state competition yet!

"Okay... I guess."

"Practice! I hear your house has a gymnasium."

"Has she been stalking you?" Rajesh asked quietly, and unfortunately, that did *not* go well.

"Who just said that?!" Mrs. Félicité screamed. She took a deep breath to calm herself. "Anyways, practice! AND MAKE SURE WHOEVER

ASKED THAT POINTLESS QUESTION DOESN'T DO THAT AGAIN!"

"Um... okay. Sorry about that," I said quickly, glaring at Rajesh at the same time. He looked at me nervously.

"I have to go," I said. I hung up quickly.

"Is she a stalker?" Rajesh asked again.

"No, Dad must have told her something. Also, be careful next time!"

"Okay... sorry, I-"

"Hey, why aren't you two asleep?" Christina interrupted, hurrying inside the room.

"Um..." I glanced at the clock which said 9:00 PM.

"You should be asleep, you have to wake up really early tomorrow!"

"Why?" I asked.

"Didn't your father tell you?"

"Tell us what?"

"Your first day of school is tomorrow!"

Three

"Our first day of school is *when*?!" I gasped in shock.

"Tomorrow! They expect you to go to the school by 7:37 in the morning, which means you have to be awake at 5:30 AM and ready by 6:17 AM, because the drive is 45 minutes from here."

"Don't you think we'll be a little too early? At that rate, we'll arrive by around 7:05," Rajesh said.

"*7:03* to be precise," Christina said. "Besides, it's best to be punctual!" I hate to admit it, but she did have a point. Punctuality is always a good thing.

"You're right," I said.

"So, you will be enrolling in the International School of Immigrants."

"The *what*?!" I asked, pretty sure I just heard the most ridiculous thing ever. "International School of Immigrants... or the ISI. You will enroll because you and your brother are immigrants, and your academic-" Rajesh didn't give her a chance to complete her sentence.

"Okay, seriously? We live here in the US. We don't need to learn English. We're already fluent!" He countered angrily.

"Yeah, but you're still counted as an immigrant."

"I've heard of immigrants who didn't go there," I pointed out quickly, mainly to get out of this.

"Oh really? Name one," Christina challenged us. I thought about it for a minute.

"I thought so," she said, when I didn't answer.

"Mrs. Félicité!" I said quickly, remembering that our acrobatics teacher was born and raised in France but went to a school in Chicago when she was our age. She told me herself when I first enrolled in my old school.

"Okay. Well... that person you just mentioned was probably a fluent English speaker who learned English as her first language, regardless of where she was raised. You two on the other hand, were born and raised in India and learned two other languages before English, and besides-"

"We can still speak fluent English!" I said. "And even if we *didn't* live in the US, we were taught English by our teachers.

"Yeah, but the headmaster still wants you both enrolling, because-"

"How does he know about us?" Rajesh asked.

"Um... I kinda *told* him about you both..." Christina muttered. Rajesh rolled his eyes and muttered,

"Of course you did."

"Okay, well, what choice have we got?" I asked. "Might as well have a positive mindset about this."

"That's the spirit! I enrolled there too, you know," Christina said.

"Really?"

"Yeah. I'm Latina, so I only spoke Spanish growing up."

"Nice," I said.

"Oh! Did you unpack already?" Christina asked, looking a little worried.

"I did... a little, I don't know about Krithi," Rajesh answered.

"No, no, no! You'll be staying there 5 days a week, and coming home over the weekend!" Christina exclaimed.

"This is a boarding school?!" Rajesh gasped.

"Yeah, why did you unpack?"

"You're the one who suggested we do so in the first place," I reminded her. "And we would've unpacked eventually, regardless of if you told us or not. Oh, and our father forgot to tell us that we were enrolling in a boarding school." I didn't want to trigger Rajesh's anxiety, so I acted calmly, but really, I was also freaking out big time.

"Oh my gosh, I'm so sorry. I'm so forgetful!" Thankfully, I didn't unpack yet.

"Okay. Rajesh, you go ahead and unpack," Christina said. "Then try on your uniform. Krithi, you can try on your uniform now."

"Okay," I said. Rajesh left the room, and I walked into that huge closet, which was actually a walk-in, found my uniform, wore it, and walked out of the closet.

"Wow!" Christina gushed. "You look awesome. Look at yourself in the mirror!" I found the mirror in the closet, and stared at myself. The uniform consisted of a navy blue skirt, which was supposed to be worn over black tights, a white tunic top, and a black blazer, which had the school's crest on it, and the school said we can do anything with our hair... as long as we're not leaving our hair down. There was an exception for hairstyles such as putting half up in a braid or ponytail. Apparently this was so that students could show their "creative side", which didn't make sense, because simple hairstyles like single ponytails were not really "creative", yet they were allowed. I decided to wear a single braid in my hair for the first day, since I am *not* doing anything too fancy that would take too much time. After admiring my uniform, I changed out into a nightgown which was hanging right next to it.

"Go ahead and get some sleep. I already set your alarm which will wake you up at the right time. Goodnight!" Christina said. I smiled at her, and I went back into the bed and fell asleep quickly.

"RISE AND SHINE!!" A voice screeched. I woke up and turned it off.

"What?! Who yelled that?" I asked, confused. The owner of the voice was nowhere to be seen! Suddenly, Christina laughed and walked in.

"Who yelled that?" I repeated, this time a little more annoyed than ever.

"I had a professional programmer program your alarm clock to yell."

"Please change it," I said, flatly, definitely not liking the idea of waking up to a very loud voice in the morning.

"Okay. Get ready. Tea is waiting downstairs."

"Alright," I agreed. I got out of bed, brushed my teeth, took a shower, got dressed, stared at the ISI uniform, braided my hair into a single braid, and walked out. Rajesh walked out from his bedroom and I stopped walking.

"Oh... my-" I didn't complete my sentence. Rajesh was wearing... *a tuxedo*!

"Yes, I know. It is way too much. I haven't even stepped on campus, and I already hate this school," Rajesh said. "But your uniform looks nice. At least you don't have to wear a tuxedo," he added. We walked over to the kitchen on the first floor, where Christina was.

"Try this," she said. She gave me and Rajesh a cup of oddly familiar looking tea.

"It's very good," Dad complimented her.

"Not as good as *you*," Christina gushed. They shared a kiss and Rajesh and I stared at them. I raised my eyebrows. They immediately stepped away from each other in embarrassment and I stopped staring. After the tea cooled down a bit, I took a sip. Wow! It tasted just like Chai... minus the spices.

"It tastes like Chai, doesn't it?" Dad asked.

"Yeah," I said. "Just... without the spices."

"It's English Breakfast tea, or black milk tea. My favorite," Christina told me. "I added a twist to it, so that it was less boring."

"What did you put in it?" Dad asked.

"Oh the twist? My secret," Christina said, smiling.

"It's really good," I said. After we finished our tea, Dad and Christina drove us to the ISI. The ISI was a huge school that could have been at least a thousand stories tall.

"I'll see you on the weekend," Dad said. He hugged us both.

"Bye." Rajesh and I walked inside the school. Oh my gosh! The interior was beautiful, but before we could grasp any other details of the school, the headmaster greeted us... or more like interrogated us.

"Names," said the headmaster, who had a name tag saying Mr. Chang.

"Krithi Sridhar, Rajesh Sridhar," we said.

"Where do you come from?"

"Atlantic City, New Jersey."

"Where were you born?"

"Amaravati, Andhra Pradesh, India."

"How old are you?"

"14 years." After at least a hundred more questions, we were finally admitted into the school.

"You'll be staying in the Asia Wing."

"Asia Wing?" I asked.

"All Asians stay there," Mr. Chang said, walking and motioning us to follow him. He led us to our dormitories. Mine was on the 7th floor, and Rajesh's was on the 8th.

"Here you are," he said to me, pointing to my assigned dormitory. I walked into it and Mr. Chang followed me.

"Hui Ying, here's the second roommate you wanted," he said. A girl who I assumed was Hui Ying said something in a different language, and Mr. Chang replied back, then left quickly, leading Rajesh to his dormitory.

"Hi!" Hui Ying said to me.

"Hi," I said. "I'm Krithi."

"Nice to meet you. I'm Hui Ying, as you know by now, and that's Chathura." She pointed to a girl who was writing in a notebook.

"Nice to meet you," Chathura said, not looking up from her notebook.

"Where are you-" I began, but Chathura interrupted me.

"I was born in Sri Lanka, my family and I lived there for who knows how long, they moved to Santa Monica, I moved to another location, and then moved to Santa Monica. I'm fluent in Sinhala and English. I'm bilingual."

"Nice," I said. "Wait... what do you mean by 'they' moved to Santa Monica and you moved to a different location? Didn't your family move with you to that location?"

"No, *I* moved to another location. Where are you from?" I didn't think she wanted to be questioned about that, so I decided to answer her other question.

"I was born in India, lived there for 7 years, moved to Atlantic City, lived there for another 7 years, then moved here. I am fluent in Telugu, Hindi, and English, meaning I'm trilingual. What about you, Hui Ying?"

"Born in China, moved here when I was 5. I'm fluent in Mandarin, Cantonese, and English, making me trilingual as well. Mr. Chang and I speak in Mandarin all the time. Also you may think this school is for learning English but it's not. To get in, you have to have good academic performance in other schools. Isn't that how your brother got in, Chathura?" Chathura nodded and said,

"Yeah, he excelled in almost every subject in school back in Sri Lanka... except for English. He didn't know any English there, so he barely passed that grade. When he moved to Santa Monica, he studied English on his own, and this school saw his academic performance and suggested he study here. He agreed and now he goes here."

"Besides that, you can take an entrance exam and they'll admit you."

"I had no idea," I said. "My father's girlfriend told the school about me and my brother and we were immediately enrolled."

"Well, your father must've talked to her and showed her a copy of both of your academic record, then she must've shown it to Mr. Chang."

"Wow," I said. I studied the look of our dormitory. It had three beds, one for each of us. The room had three separate desks, and had a couch inside as well. It also had three changing rooms for each of us, and a private restroom with a cascade shower in it. Talk about being luxurious!

"Well, we've got breakfast in, like, 5 minutes, so let's get moving," Chathura suggested. We made our way down to the 4th floor for breakfast, where we found a huge food court with multiple cafés. It was square shaped, each side having shops meant for one type of meal: breakfast, lunch, dinner, and anything extra. We went to the breakfast side and went to separate cafés. Since I only had tea this morning, I decided to get something, and I wasn't exactly close friends with Chathura or Hui Ying yet, so I didn't go with them.

"Krithi!" A voice gasped behind me.

"Rajesh?" I turned around and saw my brother at the entrance of the café I was at.

"Hi. You'll never believe who I got stuck- I mean, got put with, in my dormitory." Rajesh clearly didn't like the concept of dormitories.

"Who?" I asked.

"Alan from Kazakhstan, Tianyu from China, and Nimol from Cambodia," he explained. "Tianyu is really annoying and dramatic, Alan is straightforward and tries to look at all of the flaws in my personality, and I guess Nimol is nice."

"Oh nice. I'm with Hui Ying from China, and Chathura from Sri Lanka. They're both really kind."

"That's cool." We went to order our food then found a table in the ginormous food court. I didn't eat the scone I had got. I just stared at it. It was difficult for me to make friends in general, and I can't imagine making friends now.

"Krithi, are you okay?" Rajesh asked, knocking me out of my thoughts.

"Yeah, I'm fine," I lied, then remembered Rajesh's lecture about him being my twin brother and being able to figure out anything. He didn't say anything though... and I was glad of that.

"Get to your classes!" Mr. Chang screeched from somewhere, and I jumped when I realized that he was right next to us. "Krithi, Rajesh, here are your schedules." He lowered his voice and gave us our schedules, which he had printed and laminated.

"I have my Elective class first," I said.

"Same here," Rajesh said "And it looks like we were assigned the same elective... art." Apparently our elective had all sorts of arts, including culinary and drama. We walked to Mr. Singh's classroom and found places at cooking stations.

"Krithi Sridhar, Rajesh Sridhar, welcome," Mr. Singh said.

"Hi," we said.

"We are going to make French pastries today," Mr. Singh said. "Today, we are making chouquettes." We got the ingredients for them and began to make the round choux pastries. After they were done, I glazed the tops with chocolate glaze.

"Krithi, those chouquettes look perfect!" Mr. Singh gushed as I was still glazing them. He tried one and his face lit up. "And they taste even better!" The reason I was able to make perfect chouquettes was because our maid in India and I always experimented with different recipes after she'd bought this huge cookbook that contained recipes from all over the globe, from French pastries, to Asian curries, and a lot more. The maid and I actually had a close relationship. Rajesh would've rather kept his distance, though he was nice to her, and she was kind as well.

"Looks like someone's acing her first class," Rajesh teased. I rolled my eyes at him, smiling at the same time. Mr. Singh walked over and tried one of Rajesh's strawberry glazed chouquettes and smiled.

"Very nice, Rajesh." Mr. Singh walked away and inspected the other chouquettes as I finished glazing mine.

After a long day of classes, I decided to check out if there were any extracurriculars that I was interested in. I went over to the first floor and looked at the directory. They had a dance program at the school! The studio was on the 6th floor, and I walked there to sign up for acrobatic dancing lessons.

"Sure," the instructor said after I requested to join the team. "Show me what you got." I performed a few stunts that showed her my level, such as a front and back tuck, which were both skills I needed to master before doing any advanced acrobatics routines. She smiled and said,

"Perfect! You're in! Practice is every Monday, Tuesday, Thursday and Friday!"

"Wow. Thank you!"

"Why don't you stay for this practice? You're early!"

"Oh, okay." A thought came to me right then. How did I forget?!

"I'm competing in another competition on Saturday..."

"Really?"

"Yeah."

"Aren't you from Atlantic City?"

"Yeah," I said, shocked that she knew.

"Don't be nervous, I'm not a stalker!" The instructor laughed. "Mr. Chang told me. Anyways, did you go to the Atlantic City Statewide School of Dance?"

"Yes."

"Oh! I feel so bad for you. Mrs. Félicité is so snobby!" The instructor said.

"You know her?"

"Yeah. Anytime we all competed nationally, Mrs. Félicité would be there, since Atlantic City would compete nationally. We ran into you a couple of times, actually, now that I think about it."

"That was you?" I asked, suddenly remembering the black haired woman that I'd run into a few times when going to Dallas to compete. She would always compliment the routines that my partner and I perform. Mrs. Sayuri nodded.

"I guess I can join this one... besides, it would be hard if I am in California and the rest of Mrs. Félicité's team is in New Jersey," I said. "Yes! Oh did I introduce myself, by the way? I must have forgotten. My name is Mrs. Sayuri. Oh, and there are your teammates." I whirled around to see dancers wearing pretty leotards entering the room, walking with tiny, light steps. The outfits were entirely the same for the girls, and entirely the same for the boys. The boys were wearing black shirts, and grey pants, while the girls had fancy leotards. I walked out of the studio, went into a changing room, and changed into a leotard that I had taken with me just in case. I came back, and Mrs. Sayuri said, "Everyone, this is Krithi. She'll be joining us today!" We all sat down and I stared straight ahead.

"Everyone, I have a list of partnerships for the competition. Just so you know, you have to compete with a male partner," Mrs. Sayuri continued.

"Okay," someone said. "What are you saying?"

"You will be performing routines as... *couples*!!!"

Four

"We're *what*?!" I asked, hoping I heard her wrong.

"Dancing as couples!!" Mrs. Sayuri said. "You're with Ajith."

"Oh my-" I was mid-whisper when I realized the boy next to me was whispering the same thing. We stared at each other, and I raised my eyebrows. I assumed he was Ajith, and he looked just like Chathura, just slightly different. As soon as the rest of the partners were assigned, Ajith and I stood up and began planning out our routine.

"We can try to do a routine spontaneously," he suggested, flatly.

"We can't do that. We'll mess up! I've competed in acrobatics before. I've seen people who do that. They scored really low," I informed Ajith.

"I do that all the time, though. I score high whenever I do that."

"Seriously? I can't even imagine."

"Fine."

"Okay, let's plan out our routines." We decided we would try simple, yet advanced moves.

"Hey, why don't we try a throw and catch move? You seem ready for it," Ajith said.

"Okay." I got ready, jumped into the move, and fell on my side, my heart rate becoming way faster in panic. It took no longer than two seconds for the pain to sear through my body, and it took a lot to refrain from screaming. My heart rate finally slowed down, and I sighed in relief. Ajith helped me up quickly, and I thanked him.

"Krithi, are you okay?" Mrs. Sayuri called.

"Yeah," I replied, the pain from my fall slowly fading away.

"So that's your name," Ajith said. "I was seriously thinking of calling you Ms. Notebook." I smiled at him, then felt a strange feeling all throughout my body. I felt my cheeks go red and I seriously hoped that what I feared is happening, isn't really happening.

"So the throw and catch is out of the question," he clarified, jerking me out of my thoughts. "We can replace it with… a different move."

"Sure," I muttered. We planned the rest of the routine, practiced a lot, and eventually class ended. I made my way down to the food court to get dinner.

"Krithi, I've been looking everywhere for you!" A voice called from behind me. It was Rajesh. I'd recognize that voice anywhere.

"I'm sorry. I forgot to tell you, I decided to join the acrobatics dancing team here."

"That's great!" Rajesh said. "But you'll be up against Félicité's team," he remarked, not even bothering to address her with "Mrs."

"I know. I… need to call her. I need to tell her that I can't compete on her team," I said, hesitating a little. Rajesh's eyes widened at that.

"Seriously? She's going to be so angry!"

"Correction: She's not going to be angry. SHE'S GOING TO BE FURIOUS!" I could feel my anger boiling.

"I know. It's never good when-"

"Stop making obvious things even more obvious! You don't think I know already?" I glared at Rajesh.

"Okay, okay. You don't have to get angry," he said quietly. He was right. I was being a little rude.

"You're right, I'm sorry."

"No need to apologize." We walked into a restaurant, requested our food and began to eat.

"When will you tell Félicité?"

"Later," I replied.

"Krithi!" Another voice yelled. It was Chathura. She was standing with Ajith, who waved shyly.

"Hi, Chathura."

"Ajith just told me you both got paired for the acrobatics competition!!!"

"So...?"

"Make sure you give me the love details between you both. I want to know whenever Ajith embarrasses himself." Ajith's cheeks turned a dark shade of red and he glared at Chathura, while I gasped.

"What? Why would there be any of that?" I asked quickly.

"Because," Chathura said. "You both are doing a 'couples dance'."

"Ugh. Just because Mrs. Sayuri phrased it that way, doesn't mean we're actually doing a couples dance," Ajith said as he rolled his eyes. "Sorry," he added to me. "That's just how my sister is." *Sister*! So *that's* why they look so alike! I hadn't thought about it much, but I hadn't expected them to be related. Just at that moment, my phone chimed.

Hi there! This is Mrs. Sayuri. A message appeared.

Do you want to compete? Our next competition is on Saturday, in San Jose. We drive over there on Friday evening. Just try to practice your routine a little more so that you are ready.

Yes. I think I can... and how did you get my number? I replied.

Mr. Chang gave it to me. Every student's number is written in the directory.

Okay. Thanks for letting me know. I'll see you later.

See you, star competitor!!!

"Also," Rajesh said to Chathura after my conversation with Mrs. Sayuri was over. "Are you in any extracurriculars?"

"Yeah, I'm in both choir and jazz dancing."

"Nice," I said.

"Are you and Krithi twins?" Chathura asked Rajesh, changing the topic.

"Yes."

"Oh okay. I was trying to decide between twins or best friends who annoyingly never let each other out of sight." Rajesh looked at her in confusion. Chathura's smirk grew bigger and bigger.

"What?"

"You freaked out big time when you didn't know where Krithi was. You almost cried."

"What?! I didn't 'almost cry'!" Rajesh snapped. "But yes, I did freak out a little... you saw?"

"What do you think? You were literally at the café. By the way, the food court is the worst place to go to when you're freaking out. It's crowded."

"Yeah, I learned that the *hard way*," Rajesh said.

"You've never been to a food court before?" Chathura asked.

"No, I actually never have. I mean, we... never did much back home. It was school, extracurricular, then back home."

"How come?" Ajith asked quietly.

"I..." Rajesh began. He looked at me, and I looked right back. I nodded.

"Our mother left us. After that, we stopped socializing. The only reason we'd ever socialize is for school. Our father had us take extracurriculars so that we'd take our minds off of our mother."

"I'm sorry," Ajith said to us.

"I guess it's fine. Ever since then, Dad's been dating a girl called Christina," I said. Chathura's and Ajith's eyes widened.

"You know her?" I asked.

"Gonzalez, right?" Chathura asked.

"I think," I said.

"Christina used to be our neighbor until she got rich and left the neighborhood," Ajith said. "Also, our dad used to work with her."

"Wow... how did she get so rich?" I asked.

"I think she has a very high quality job or something." We finished eating and then Chathura and I walked up to our dormitory, where we saw Hui Ying painting. I looked at her canvas. She was painting a pier and a sunset, perfectly capturing every bit and piece. Every little detail. Every shop at the pier. Every wave of the water.

"Is that the Santa Monica Pier?" Chathura asked.

"Yeah! Do you like it?" Hui Ying asked.

"I love it!" I said.

"During weekends and summer break, my sisters, brother and I always go over to the Santa Monica Pier, just us four."

"That's cool," Chathura said. "But isn't your brother, like, your Irish twin? Why didn't you go with your parents?"

"They work long hours... and besides, my sisters are adults already. We live right near the pier."

"Oh." Chathura shrugged.

"Does your brother go here?" I asked.

"Yeah. He stays with this student called Rajesh. Apparently he's like, the worst person to stay with. He's arrogant, isolated, and straightforward, but at the same time, he's over emotional." Chathura and I exchanged looks.

"Hui Ying, Rajesh is my brother," I said, trying to contain my anger. "And what you said was not true at all."

"Oh, I'm sorry. I didn't know. Uh... maybe Tianyu was talking about a different Rajesh?"

"No... Rajesh told me he was in a dormitory with your brother," I said, frowning.

"Okay. It's a little more likely that Tianyu was overexaggerating. He's known for that. As his older sister, it's my duty to make sure he doesn't get into arguments with others due to him being overdramatic. I'm so sorry, I did not mean to offend you."

"It's okay, you didn't know," I said. "Wait, you're older? Isn't he your twin?"

"Irish twin," Hui Ying corrected, hanging her picture up, as well as putting away her paints and brushes.

"Do you know what an Irish twin is?" Chathura asked me. I hated to admit it but...

"No, I don't."

"Oh, okay. An Irish twin is basically a sibling who was born in the same year as you, but it isn't on the same day. For example, Hui Ying was born on February 10th, while Tianyu was born later that year on November 12."

"Oh okay. Thanks." My phone buzzed and I checked it. It was Rajesh. *Did you talk to Félicité about competing?* Oh great, I forgot! I immediately called Mrs. Félicité.

"Well, if it isn't the famous Krithi Sridhar." Her voice boomed from the phone.

"Yeah?"

"You know, everyone's been talking about you. Since you moved. Saying how much they miss-"

"Whatever." I knew Mrs. Félicité was being sarcastic, and I didn't care.

"Anyway, I joined a new acrobatics program. The ISI-"

"YOU JOINED ISI'S ACROBATICS CLASS?!" Mrs. Félicité's voice was louder than ever.

"Yes. I joined ISI's acrobatics class, and I'm competing with them in the Statewide competition." I tried to stay calm but it was hard not to freak out in fear that Mrs. Félicité might say something derogatory.

"Okay. Well, good luck, but my competitors are unstoppable. Even if you miraculously make it to Nationals, with the way my dancers have been dancing now, you and the rest of Sayuri's so-called team don't have a chance of medaling."

"Didn't they medal last year?"

"Yeah, some boy on Sayuri's team. I think he's from South Asia. He got a silver medal with his routine, but I could tell he didn't plan it. How'd he score so high? The judges must've favored him. Do you know him, by the way? I believe his name's Ajith or something-" And at that moment, Chathura, who was eavesdropping the whole time, decided that she'd had enough. She sprung off her bed and marched over to mine. Quickly, she snatched my phone out of my hands and held it to her face as she snapped,

"Yes. He's Krithi's partner in the competition. And he's a great acrobatic dancer, so if he doesn't match up to your standards, that's your problem!" I widened my eyes at her. Since when does Chathura disrespect her elders?

"Chathura!" I said quietly and angrily at the same time. She shrugged and handed me my phone back, looking satisfied with herself.

"He's your partner?" Mrs. Félicité asked. Surprisingly, she was calmer than expected and didn't mention a thing about what Chathura had said. "Woah. Uh... okay, you might medal! Bye!" She tried to hang up but I stopped her.

"Wait!" I said. "How did you come to know you were going to Nationals?"

"Oh that was a guess." She hung up immediately and I blinked in confusion. Why did she want to hang up so quickly?

"Let's... sleep. Shall we? That... was a long few minutes," Hui Ying suggested. I nodded.

"Sure." We fell asleep within minutes and before I knew it, my alarm rang again the next morning.

I walked downstairs to the food court, where I saw the dancers in the acrobatics program seated, eating pastries and having tea. They were the only ones in the food court besides me. As soon as they saw me, half of them started whispering and one walked up to me.

"Good. You're here."

"Um-"

"We didn't introduce ourselves yesterday. My name's Vanessa. I'm from Austria." Another girl stepped forward.

"My name's Araceli. I'm from Spain." A third girl stepped forward.

"My name's Sienna and I'm from Italy." The others slowly introduced themselves.

"By the way, Mrs. Sayuri told us about you being on Félicité's team. I'm sorry you had to deal with her," Vanessa said.

"Yeah," A girl called Gabriella from Columbia agreed.

"Félicité's weird," A girl called Luisa from Germany said.

"Not as weird as this guy I room with," A boy said as he walked up to us.

"Sorry I'm late." He turned to me. "Alan, from Kazakhstan. You?" The name sounded familiar.

"Um... Krithi, from India. My brother is in the same dormitory as you," I said.

"Oh, Rajesh? He's arrogant, isolated and straightforward-" he began, but stopped when he saw that I was glaring at him.

"He is not!" I snapped in frustration. "Well, he can be isolated... but not those other qualities you said!!"

"Okay, calm down. He's not the weird guy I was mentioning, just so you know."

"Who's the weird one then?" Sienna asked.

"Tianyu," Alan said. "I think his sister also goes to this school-"

"Yeah. Hui Ying. She is in my dormitory," I said, stopping him mid sentence.

"She's probably double weird."

"No. She's actually really nice," I said, frowning. I could tell that he was quick to jump to conclusions, and I did *not* like that about him.

"Okay. Whatever you say," Alan said. He continued ranting about Tianyu and I didn't bother to listen.

"Churro?" Araceli offered me something thick and fried coated in cinnamon and sugar, and a small cup of chocolate sauce. "It's meant to be dipped in there. It's the best," she explained. I dipped the churro in the rich chocolate and took a bite. Immediately I was able to taste the fluffy cake-like texture of the churro, along with the sugar and cinnamon and the chocolate.

"This is good!" I complimented her.

"Thanks!" Araceli said. "I love it. It's a Spanish dessert. The restaurant made a twist to an original recipe, and it's quite unique." I wasn't able to tell because I had never actually had a churro before until now. I didn't say that, though. I remained quiet as everyone else selected pastries.

"You can get anything you want! All these foods we have here are native to our cultures," Sienna said. She pointed to a few pastries laid out on a plate. I looked at everything until I spotted a muffin.

"I'll just take this," I said, taking the muffin. After I put it on a plate, I poured myself a cup of black tea and sat down in silence. We ate until our first class, which today, for me, was history.

"I've got history," I said to the others.

"Same here," Vanessa, Sienna and Araceli said at the same time. We walked to the classroom together.

"Hi, Mrs. Albrecht," Araceli said.

"Araceli, Vanessa, and Sienna! You three are late!" Mrs. Albrecht barked.

"What?! It's only by a minute," Araceli pointed out, and Sienna and Vanessa stared at her and said simultaneously,

"Araceli!"

"Sorry, Mrs. Albrecht," Vanessa said, politely. "We will try to be on time next time."The three of them sat down at their desks, which, I assumed, were far away from each other. I hadn't seen Mrs. Albrecht in my last history class though, which was strange.

"You!" Mrs. Albrecht added once she saw me. "I've never seen you in my class."

"Oh no," Sienna said.

"Zip it, Sienna. You're already late. Don't break another rule," Mrs. Albrecht snapped. "Now back to you," she added to me. "Why have you never been in this class before?"

"Um..." I didn't get a chance to say anything, because I caught a glimpse of Sienna as she whispered something to Vanessa, who facepalmed.

"Mrs. Albrecht-" Vanessa began, but Mrs. Albrecht cut her off mid sentence.

"What's the problem here?"

"This is Europe Wing's history class. Krithi is supposed to be in the Asia Wing."

"Oh, that's your name. Okay, well, hurry along!" I bolted out of there and made my way to the Asia Wing, where our history teacher, Mrs. Keo, was frowning at me.

"Krithi, you're *late*."

"I know. I went to Europe Wing's history class by mistake. I'm so sorry. I won't make that mistake again." Mrs. Keo glared at me for two more seconds, then sighed.

"I'll make an exception, only because the wings are confusing and this is only your second day here. The next time you are late, it's a week of detention." *Detention*?! A full *week*?! For being *late*? Mrs. Keo must've read my mind because she added,

"We enforce a lot of discipline in the Asia Wing classes, just so you are aware."

"Understood," I said quickly. I was generally a responsible student who was always on time, so I was quite embarrassed that I was late this time.

"Okay, now get to your desk," she told me. I nodded and I walked over to my desk and jumped. Ajith was sitting right next to it. He flashed me a smile, and I smiled back. I felt my cheeks go red and I shook my head. I sat down awkwardly and quietly.

"All right. Open your textbooks to Page 35, and read about the topic," Mrs. Keo instructed. I opened my textbook and began reading about the American Revolution. I was reading for so long, that when the bell rang, I didn't even notice, until I felt someone shaking me.

"Krithi!" I looked over to who shook me. It was Chathura.

"What?" I asked, annoyed that she had shaken me in the first place.

"You know, class ended, like, 10 minutes ago, right?" Ajith said.

"Really?" I asked. I read the clock. 9:50.

"We've still got 10 minutes of our break left," Hui Ying said.

"Yeah. Let's go to the food court and get something to eat. You look famished," Chathura said.

"Not really," I mumbled as I packed my things and left, with a suspicious Mrs. Keo looking back at us. I walked over to the shops in the food court.

"Krithi! You'd better come quick!" Chathura yelled.

"What happened?" I turned around and gasped. I saw a panicked Rajesh crying and panting. It was uncontrollable and all eyes were on us. I was the only one who knew what was happening, which meant I was the only one who could fix it.

Five

"Rajesh, listen to me," I said, walking over to him and putting my hand on his shoulder. He continued trembling, but was able to manage a weak nod.

"Close your eyes," I whispered. He did as I asked and remained silent. "Focus on breathing, okay? Think about all of the positive stuff that's been happening. We met new friends! We're attending a very good school. We're lucky to be here." Rajesh nodded again as he slowly stopped trembling. He stopped crying and he looked up. He smiled weakly and whispered,

"Thank you." I threw my arms around him, fighting back tears. It had been a while since I'd seen Rajesh have a panic attack. Something intense must've happened. He rubbed my back slowly. He knew that it was scary to watch him in that phase. He looked so vulnerable to his emotions, which unfortunately, was the truth in that moment.

"What happened?" I asked as we sat down somewhere along with Chathura and Ajith.

"You may not like it," he answered as he looked at me worriedly.

"Rajesh, you are going to need to tell me if it causes you to panic like this. Remember what we agreed on?" I reminded him.

"Fine. Our *mother* just sent me a text message... somehow. She heard we enrolled in this school. She just can't do this!" Rajesh was two seconds away from crying again.

"Do what?" I asked, gently. I tried to remain calm, but whenever our mother was brought up in a discussion, it was hard not to freak out.

"She asked if we were in any extracurriculars. I said that I wasn't, and I mentioned that you were in acrobatics. She wanted to come to your next competition, which is soon, and she didn't take no for an answer, so I guess we're seeing her again." As soon as Rajesh had finished speaking, I covered my mouth in shock. The tears I was fighting back streamed down my face, but before I could try to wipe them away, Chathura and Ajith noticed. They wrapped their arms around me as I cried until the next class.

"I knew you'd hate it," Rajesh muttered as I got up and started walking to my next class.

"I don't get it. Just because I'm in acrobatics, she now wants to see us. See us for our extracurriculars. For our accomplishments. SHE DOESN'T WANT TO SEE US FOR OURSELVES, FOR OURSELVES!" I yelled.

"Hey, calm down! I understand how it feels, but for a person with anxiety, I know what is bad and what's not. You can thank Maria for that."

"Really?" I asked, remembering the therapist Rajesh used to talk to back in Atlantic City. He nodded and I smiled a little. Maria was very kind to Rajesh. She helped him a lot with his anxiety, and he is a lot better than he was when he was first diagnosed, thanks to her. I really liked her.

"You should probably talk to Maria about this when you next see her," I suggested.

"NO! DEFINITELY NOT!! ARE YOU OUT OF YOUR MIND?! THAT WON'T SOLVE ANYTHING!" Rajesh yelled, looking angrier than he'd ever looked before. I was shocked, but I understood at the same time. He has sudden bursts of anger at times, but still, it was shocking. He then noticed my reaction and lowered his volume. "This is personal."

"Okay, then." I hurried over to the next class, trying to forget what just happened.

***

"Hi, Krithi! Hi, Ajith!" Mrs. Sayuri said later that day in acrobatics, when Ajith and I arrived at the gymnasium. "You're early!"

"Just practicing a little extra," I said, stretching a little.

"Okay." As I started to get into a position for a front tuck, my mother suddenly came into my mind, and I fell on my knees after the move.

"I don't understand. You were able to do it before," Ajith said, his hand outstretched. I grabbed it and looked at the ground.

"I don't know. I just... fell, I guess." Ajith looked at me concernedly for another second before asking,

"Is this about your mother?"

"No. I don't care. Not anymore," I lied.

"What happened? Are you okay?" Mrs. Sayuri asked.

"I don't want to talk about it," I said, frowning. The last thing I wanted was for more people to know what happened.

"Okay," Mrs. Sayuri said. "I hope you're alright, though." The rest of the acrobatics team came into the studio and sat down.

"I hope your brother's okay," Vanessa whispered to me.

"Yeah," Araceli agreed.

"We saw what happened," Sienna informed me. "Is he alright?"

"Yes, he's fine. Thanks for asking."

"What happened, though?" Araceli asked. "I've never seen that happen before."

"Shut up, Araceli," Alan snapped from somewhere.

"What did I do now?" Araceli growled back.

"She's got a lot on her shoulders right now. Asking her questions would only make things worse," Alan said, approaching us. I looked down at the ground and didn't say a word.

"I'm only curious. She doesn't have to tell us if she doesn't want to," Araceli told us.

"It's personal," I finally said. "I don't think he wants anyone to know besides us... and nor do I."

"See?" Alan said.

"I didn't know! Honestly I don't get why you hate me so much. I clearly did nothing to you!" Araceli yelled.

"Nothing?" Alan asked.

"Nothing," Araceli replied.

"Don't say you didn't do anything. You did awful things!" Alan screamed.

"Like *what*? I talked badly about your sister?" Araceli sneered. Alan glared at her. Araceli's facial expression became serious like it was before.

"No, I didn't. I already told you-"

"Can you two break it up?" Mrs. Sayuri asked. "Or else, you both are *out of my class.*"

"Fine," Araceli said. I looked at the ground and didn't speak until we were instructed to split into our groups and practice our routines. I failed a back tuck for the second time, falling on the mat.

"Are you sure you are okay?" Ajith asked.

"Yes." He sighed. After a few seconds, he said,

"Okay, you're clearly lying to me. You keep falling and I'm worried about you. Chathura is even more worried about you, and she won't stop asking me if you're okay." He sat down beside me on the mat.

"I'm fine," I lied as I stood up. I walked up to Mrs. Sayuri. "Can I leave, please?"

"Sure. I can tell you have a lot on your plate. Come back on Thursday, okay?"

"Okay." I walked out and went over to my dormitory. I was the only one there. Hui Ying had extracurricular art class, and Chathura had jazz dancing. Every emotion that I was holding back suddenly came out of me. I cried and cried until I was able to stop, and I was so relieved no one was there. After calming down, I worked on homework until dinner. I walked over to the food court and stared at the options. I felt a tap on my shoulder. I turned behind me. It was Rajesh.

"Hey," he said. "I just wanted to say I am so sorry for the way I reacted earlier. You had a point when you suggested I talk to Maria about what happened, and I will."

"Really? Okay, and it's fine," I said.

"You sure?"

"Yeah. Definitely," I assured him. He smiled nervously and walked away to another shop.

"Hey Krithi," Vanessa's voice said from behind me.

"Hi, Vanessa," I said. "Are you okay?" Her eyes were fear stricken and she looked nervous.

"I am, but Sienna's not."

"What happened?" I asked, very aware that whatever went on happened *after* I left acrobatics.

"You know how Sienna and Alan are partners, right?" Vanessa said.

"Well, after you left, Sienna tried to do a really advanced move. She fell, and Alan got mad at her for going too above her level."

"Oh no, is she okay?"

"You would've thought so, considering she fell on a mat, but she and Alan argued and eventually, uh, Alan pushed Sienna, and she fell on the floor. Then Alan began beating her up more, and now Sienna is in the nurse's office, and Alan's suspended from acrobatics classes."

"What, really?!" I gasped. I didn't know Alan could get so physical.

"Krithi, what did Vanessa tell you?" Alan came up behind us as we walked into a restaurant.

"Vanessa told me that you beat Sienna up!" I snapped.

"What?! Why would I ever do that? Vanessa, why did you tell her that?"

"Well you did," Vanessa said.

"No. No I didn't. Do me a favor, will you? Stop lying and turning almost every new student against me."

"Okay fine, Araceli did want me to turn Krithi against you by pretending that you hurt Sienna, but I didn't want to do it, I swear," Vanessa told Alan.

"Why would you do it then?" I asked.

"It's sort of like we're servants to Araceli. We're only her friends to serve her and other stuff. It's hard to get out of it."

"Wow, that's terrible," I said, getting food and heading to a table. A few minutes later, Vanessa and Alan joined me at the table.

"So now you know?" Vanessa said. "I am so sorry. Araceli-"

"I get it," Alan told her quickly. "Araceli is persuasive. That's why I hate her. And... sorry, I guess, for the way I reacted to that."

"It's... okay."

"She's been pretending to be friendly?" I asked.

"Yeah. I was never suspended, and Sienna did try that move, but I wasn't angry," Alan said. "In fact, Sienna was upset about it, and I tried to help her perfect it. Araceli's horrible."

"We should bust her," Vanessa suggested.

"Don't you think that's going to make her upset?" I asked.

"What did she just do to us?" Vanessa asked.

"Krithi's right," Sienna's voice came from behind us. I gasped as Sienna joined us, a plate of food in her hand.

"What did you hear?" The three of us asked at the same time.

"Everything. Don't worry," she added when she saw our worried faces. "I'm not going to bust you or anything, and I agree with you, Krithi. As much as I hate Araceli, busting her would only provoke her to do more."

"Okay then. Let's finish eating," Alan said. We finished eating and then headed to our dormitories. Chathura and Hui Ying were waiting there.

"Hi," Hui Ying said. "Want to head down to the Asia Wing common room?"

"We have common rooms?" I asked.

"Yeah. If we want to hang out with others from the Asia Wing, we can hang out there," Chathura said.

"Okay," I said. We three walked over to the Asia Wing common room, which happened to be a wide room with couches and other things. I spotted Rajesh concernedly talking to Ajith. Those two seemed to have clicked.

"HUI YING, IT IS SO GOOD TO SEE YOU!!!" A girl's voice yelled loudly, so Hui Ying and Chathura went over to whoever it was. I looked around until I heard a familiar voice say,

"Hey, Krithi." The voice came from behind me, so I turned around and found Ajith.

"Hi," I said.

"How are you?" I knew he was referring to the moment where I left acrobatics quickly and suddenly, but I wasn't going to admit the truth.

"I'm fine. How was acrobatics after I left?"

"Acrobatics was fine," Ajith said. We walked over to a table.

"So... are you okay now?" He asked, looking at me concernedly.

"Just fine," I lied. Ajith looked around. Then, he put his hand on my arm.

"Is something wrong?" I asked, since he looked concerned.

"You know, Rajesh told me he yelled at you. He's really sorry. As much as you forgave him, he still feels really upset about that. He didn't mean anything." I placed my hand on my forehead. I felt awful that Rajesh felt this way! I had no idea that it made him so guilty.

"I should probably talk to him," I said.

"You should," Ajith agreed. "I mean, he didn't really listen to me, given the fact that he barely knows me. Maybe he will listen to you?"

"Yeah." I walked over to Rajesh, who was looking down. I sat down on the couch, which was oddly too soft.

"Hey," I said. "Are you okay?"

"No. I... feel horrible."

"It's okay," I told him.

"No, it's not. In fact... there's something I kind of... have to tell you."

"What is it?" I asked, gently.

"Dad gave me Maria's number so I spoke to her about 15 minutes ago. She told me she wants to talk to you."

"Me?" I asked. "Why?" Rajesh looked carefully at me.

"Are you sure you want to know this?" I pondered this for a couple of seconds, then said,

"Yes." Rajesh hesitated. Then, he said,

"She thinks you're developing anxiety."

Six

"She thinks I'm developing *anxiety*?!" I gasped, widening my eyes. Of course, there was nothing *wrong* with anxiety, but I never knew I'd have it. My anger started boiling quickly.

"It's just a guess. She wants to talk to you so that she can find out what the truth is," Rajesh tried to explain but I didn't listen to him.

"Seriously?!" I yelled. "I don't have anxiety!"

"Krithi, calm down," Ajith said, as he rested his hands gently on my shoulders. "Please, just calm down."

"No! I can't believe Maria thinks I have anxiety!" This was the angriest I've ever been, and I wasn't able to calm down and figure out why.

"Krithi, it's normal," Ajith said, soothingly. "I know many people who have anxiety."

"I DO NOT-"

"Krithi, please!" Ajith tried to warn me. "You're going to say things you don't want to say!" He was too late. My anger had already reached a point where I had no more patience.

"I'M NOT MY BROTHER!" I screamed. All eyes fell on me immediately. Rajesh looked shocked, Ajith covered his mouth, and Chathura and Hui Ying looked at me in a way they never have before. Their friend stared at me too. I looked over at Rajesh and immediately realized my mistake. I gasped.

"Rajesh, I-" He shook his head.

"It's fine." He was lying. I could see the shock on his face. "Maria's coming here. Tomorrow evening. She booked her flight already so there's no turning back."

"Okay. I'm so sorry. I don't know what I was saying. Is there anything I can do to make it up to you?"

"You were angry. I've made similar mistakes when we were younger to a lot of people."

"Rajesh-" I began, but he held his hand up to stop me.

"Now I know for a fact that you do need to speak to her, though. She can help you with your temper." I looked at him apologetically, and he stared straight ahead. I began walking away slowly and left the common room as soon as I could.

The next day was a very uneventful one, and before I knew it, I found myself in a room with Maria.

"Good to see you, Krithi," she said. I stayed silent and looked at the ground.

"Listen. Rajesh told me what happened. I'm only here to ask some questions."

"Okay, but first, why did you fly here *just* to speak to me? That's pointless. It honestly isn't a big deal and regardless, I could've gotten your number instead." It took me three seconds to realize that I actually said that and I winced in shock. I cannot believe I spoke without thinking. *Again*!

"I didn't fly here just to see you. I am also here to see a friend," Maria told me quietly. I looked at her and said,

"Oh my gosh. I am so sorry, I didn't mean to say anything like that!"

"It's alright, things happen. Anyways, I'm curious, have you been feeling anxious lately?"

"No," I said.

"Okay... then, Rajesh said you burst out and said that you weren't him." I stared at the ground for a few seconds.

"I did," I admitted eventually.

"Why?"

"I... wasn't thinking straight. I spoke without thinking, and I seriously regret what happened."

"Okay." Maria looked at me for two seconds and then asked,

"Have you ever felt really hyper?"

"No," I said, confused.

"Okay, you probably just have mood swings or a short temper. Has your mood ever shifted randomly?"

"Definitely," I said.

"Okay. Oh, and there's no diagnosis, if that's what you're worried about."

"How could you tell?"

"I'm a therapist. I know things."

"I'm so glad!" I said. "But... really?"

"Yeah," Maria shrugged. "It seems like you just have a short temper. Honestly, that's something many people have, and it's no one's fault.

You're fine."

"How do I apologize to Rajesh for that awful thing I said?"

"You apologized already, right? He'll come around. These things happen. Everyone makes mistakes. If there is something I know about your brother, he'll definitely forgive you, but he will still be a little angry and hide his feelings. Don't be shocked about it and for now I encourage you to focus on something else." I shrugged. After a few more questions and some advice, our session was thankfully done.

"See you another time," Maria said. We left the room and I headed over to my dormitory. That's when Hui Ying gave me a text.

Come to the Asia Wing common room. NOW. Ajith is in a really bad mood, just know that. He wants to talk to you about what happened yesterday.

I did not feel good about that, but it was probably important, and besides, it was probably inevitable. I hurried over to the common room where I found Ajith, Chathura and Hui Ying sitting at a table. Chathura saw me first and motioned for me to come over. I went over to them. Ajith stared at his hands on a table, Chathura looked at the table, and Hui Ying looked as if she was trying to find the right words to say. I sat down awkwardly and stared at the floor.

"So... how'd your session go?" Hui Ying asked.

"Not bad," I said. "Maria is really nice, actually."

"Okay, but we actually are curious... why did you yell at Rajesh like that?"

"I didn't mean to-" I began, but I was stopped mid sentence by Ajith.

"I told you Krithi. I told you that you'd say things you don't wish to say," he said, sternly.

"I know," I admitted quietly.

"And it was just for a simple diagnosis, that too!" Ajith snapped. "One that a lot of people have!" I couldn't take it anymore. Everything that I've been trying to control inside of me just exploded.

"I didn't want to have to deal with another diagnosis! Especially since I had to go through a *lot* when I had my old one! The thing is, Rajesh's diagnosis was probably worse than mine, and I was terrified about what would happen to me, so I burst out. When he got diagnosed, that was the worst for my family. In fact, that's probably the reason my mother left us. She didn't want to stay with a child who had a diagnosis, especially a mental one." The others looked at each other and then back at me.

"You've had a diagnosis?" Ajith asked, softly. He got up, moved next to me, and looked at me, concerned. I looked straight ahead.

"I was diagnosed with depression. I hid it from our mother, since she was already dealing with a lot. Rajesh didn't hide his diagnosis. He thought he could get the right support from our mother, while I chose to go to our father instead, who already knew about mine and Rajesh's," I said, holding back tears.

"Are you sure that's the real reason your mother left?" Hui Ying asked.

"She left soon after Rajesh told her about his anxiety. Seems like it," I told her. Ajith looked at me for a few seconds, then said,

"I can see why you said that to him now."

"There isn't an excuse," I said. "I never should've said that."

"Wait. If she left *because* of him, then how come your mother checked in with Rajesh yesterday?"

"It's probably because she was around her new husband."

"Your stepdad?" Hui Ying asked.

"Yes... technically, but I will never call him that. She probably wanted to show him that she 'cared' about her children." I felt the tears that I was holding back run down my face. I quickly wiped them away as my friends gave me looks of deep concern.

"Rajesh doesn't even think that the reason my mother left was because of his diagnosis."

"Really? Well if you told him-" Ajith began.

"No. Rajesh will get deeply hurt."

"With what?" A familiar voice asked. I heard footsteps and next thing I knew, my brother was standing next to my chair. I turned around.

"I... Rajesh, I'm so sorry-"

"I know. Just tell me what happened."

"Nothing," I lied. He raised his eyebrows.

"You know how you asked if you can make what you said up to me? This is how. Tell me what happened. It's clearly serious,"

"I- okay, but later-"

"I feel like you've been keeping secrets for years now. 7 to be precise. Just tell me. Please," Rajesh said. Ajith looked at me, then nodded.

"Okay. Um... we shouldn't do this here."

"How about that room?" He pointed to a room that was straight ahead

"Sure..." I said. We walked over to the room and sat down. The room consisted of cream colored walls, chintz armchairs, and a picture of Mr. Chang framed in gold. It actually looked as if we were in a headmaster's office.

"What happened?" Rajesh asked, jerking me out of my thoughts.

"Uh... okay. I-" I couldn't hurt my brother like this. I've hurt him enough.

"Take your time," he said.

"Um... I can't do it," I said. "Look, it's a secret hidden for a while, I just don't think revealing it would be a good idea, don't you think?" Rajesh sighed. He hesitated for a second. I wondered what was going on in his mind.

"I promise not to get angry with you." It was a lie, but I sort of realized that it was my only option. I had to tell him everything.

"Okay." I sighed. I fought back tears and explained everything. By the end of the story, Rajesh looked extremely shocked.

"I knew you'd-"

"Don't. It isn't your fault. I get why you said what you said."

"Rajesh, there's no excuse for what I said." He stayed silent for a couple of minutes.

"We should go," he suggested.

"Yeah."

"Also, just so you know, I wasn't angry with you at all. After thinking about it, I actually understood that you were revisiting what had happened to you back when you had your depression, and you were scared. You didn't mean it. I was just... shocked." I smiled slightly, he returned it, and we walked out, Rajesh walked out of the common room and Hui Ying, Chathura, and Ajith came over to me.

"So did you explain?" Ajith asked. I nodded.

"I'm so sorry this whole thing happened," Hui Ying whispered. Chathura smiled a comforting smile.

"It's fine," I said.

"Try to forget about it. Okay?" Ajith said, placing his hand on my shoulder. The last thing I could do was forget about it, but I knew that Ajith wasn't going to drop it unless I agreed, so I basically had no choice but to lie.

"Okay."

Seven

I'd been so busy that I didn't even realize that time had gone by so quickly and before I knew it, we were getting ready to drive to San Jose for the acrobatics competition, which was tomorrow. I'd already informed my father and Christina back when Mrs. Sayuri informed me a few days back (who was able to register me last minute), and they're flying from the Los Angeles airport to San Jose. Rajesh is going as well, and he's going with Dad and Christina, and my *mother* had already flown from India to San Jose after informing Rajesh she's coming. "Krithi! HOW COULD YOU FORGET?" Ajith yelled at me while we left the school, after I told him that I had forgotten that our competition was tomorrow.

"I'm sorry, I was really busy," I said, getting inside the car. Some of the parents volunteered to carpool the students, and Ajith and I were in a car with his father as well as Vanessa. Since I get motion sickness, I was seated in the front seat, and after 6 hours of an uneventful car ride, we finally reached San Jose. Thank goodness for that! As soon as we went to the hotel, we divided into rooms. I'm so relieved we didn't take over the entire third floor of the hotel. There were 20 people (parents, siblings, and Mrs. Sayuri included) divided up into 5 rooms, so Vanessa, Ajith and I were in one room, along with Mrs. Sayuri.

"So..." Vanessa said.

"You ready?" Ajith asked.

"No," Vanessa answered immediately.

"We're not either," I said.

"Relax. You'll be okay. Now we should sleep, it's 1:00 in the morning. Thank goodness tomorrow's competition is in the evening, so we can sleep a little extra," Mrs. Sayuri tried to reassure us, but no amount of assurance would help us. The pressure was still on.

The next evening was crowded. First, the check in took *forever*, then we had to warm up. As soon as we were finished, we had some time to meet our parents.

"Dad!" I gasped, running over to meet him.

"Hi, Krithi."

"Good luck!" Christina said.

"Thanks."

"Krithi? Oh my goodness, I've missed you!" A horribly familiar voice said. I timidly looked behind my father, to see my mother grinning at me. I didn't speak. Rajesh quietly stood next to Christina. Dad stepped behind me (I hope he was glaring at her) and now my mother and I were face to face.

"You've grown so much!" My mother made her way to hug me, but I held my hand up to stop her. She took a step back.

"I know you're upset that I left, but it was for a good reason," she said.

"No it wasn't!" I snapped. "You left because you were scared about being humiliated! The truth is, there's nothing you can do or say to control what has happened. You *knew* that. You just left, though. You thought running away from your problems would fix things!!! IT. DOESN'T. WORK. THAT. WAY!!!" Everyone stared at us, and Ajith walked over. Tears of anger spilled down my face. I knew I wasn't exactly going by the term "respect your elders", but I couldn't help it.

"Krithi, we need to be-" he began but stopped midway. Noticing the tears on my face, he immediately made the connection. Christina looked away, Rajesh stared straight ahead, holding back his anger, my mother raised her eyebrows, Dad nodded, and Ajith stayed silent as I followed him over to the area where we were supposed to wait. As soon as we arrived to the area, he asked me,

"Are you okay?" I nodded in response as I wiped my tears and we waited as Sienna and Alan finished their round. It was our turn. I got up and we walked on stage.

"Just like we practiced, okay?" Ajith reminded me.

"Okay," I said. I had gotten a perfect balance on Ajith's hands and I was thrown in the air, and I don't know how many flips I did before he stopped me from landing and hoisted me onto his hands again. I heard a huge amount of applause and I smiled slightly. We were instructed to perform our other routines, which went perfectly. As soon as we were finished, the judges announced the winners.

"ISI will be making it to the National competition in Dallas." It took me a couple of seconds to realize what the judge had said. Then, I covered my mouth in shock.

"Krithi!!! OH MY GOSH WE MADE IT TO THE NATIONAL COMPETITION!" Vanessa screamed.

"We did it!" Sienna yelled, shaking me. I stepped back and smiled at her. Many members of the team screamed and hugged each other. I watched them and Ajith walked up to me.

"You know, you ended up using a lot of power in those flips," he said to me, smiling.

"Really?" I asked.

"Yeah," he answered. I thought about it for a couple seconds.

"Guess I was just angry," I said, crossing my arms. He smiled again, only this time it was a sympathetic one, and we went over to meet our families. Rajesh walked up to me and smiled.

"You did a great job," he said, but as soon as my mother walked up to me, his expression turned from a smile to a worried glance.

"You were awesome!!" She hugged me and I didn't say a word. They both backed away from me at the same time, then looked at each other at the same time, then frowned. They turned to me.

"Don't look at me," I said. They turned to Dad, who looked at Christina, who eventually looked back at me. I rolled my eyes in annoyance.

"Krithi!" Ajith's voice said from somewhere. He walked up to us. I sighed.

"Hi," I said, flatly.

"The rest of the team wants you at the exit…" His voice trailed off as soon as he saw my mother grinning at him in a really weird way. I could tell that he was very uncomfortable, because he stared at my mother in an awkward way, and a couple seconds later, he stared at the ground. He looked at me and asked,

"Um... you know where the exit is, right?"

"Yes," I said.

"Okay, I'll meet you there. I'll tell Mrs. Sayuri that you'll be there soon." He hurried away quickly and I frowned at my mother.

"I don't think you realize the meaning of 'it doesn't work that way'," I said.

"Okay, I understand that you're angry with me, but that doesn't mean you get to act like a mad child," my mother scolded. I was two seconds away from losing my temper again, but after remembering what happened with Rajesh the other day and what happened right before the competition, I decided not to rise to my mother's bait. Instead, I told her calmly,

"First of all, I'm 14 years old, so I don't classify myself as a 'child'. Second of all, I am not being mad. I'm simply just acting normal for the situation we were put in."

"So what? It doesn't affect you!" My mother yelled.

"No, but it affects my brother," I told her, still keeping my patience. Rajesh narrowed his eyes at our mother, then looked at me gratefully.

"I have to meet the team at the exit," I said.

"Go ahead," Dad told me. I left without saying a word and ran into Vanessa.

"Sorry, Krithi! I was just coming to get you."

"It's fine," I said.

"I saw everything. Do you mind if I ask what that was all about?" I stayed quiet for a couple seconds.

"Nothing. I just have... problems with my mother," I eventually said.

"Okay, well, we're all going out for dinner as a celebration. Hopefully that'll take your mind off of that." We joined our friends and she gave me a smile. Ajith grabbed my hand sympathetically and I felt my cheeks go red. Vanessa's smile turned into a smirk, and I rolled my eyes at her. We went to a fancy restaurant that was in our hotel and ate there, then we left. After we entered our hotel room, I sat down on one of the beds. Ajith sat beside me and asked,

"Krithi, what happened with you and your mother? That was a lot of yelling, and the way-"

"I know. The smiling was weird. I'm so sorry."

"No, I'm not worried about that. The thing I'm worried about is the way you both attracted everyone's attention-" I facepalmed as soon as Ajith said that, not letting him finish speaking.

"Seriously?!" If there was anything I hated more than anything, it was unnecessary attention. There was a knock on our door.

"I'll get it." Ajith answered and found Rajesh.

"Hey. Can I come in?" He asked.

"Sure." Ajith stepped aside to let Rajesh in. Rajesh walked towards me and handed me something. I didn't look at it.

"Our mother wanted to... apologize for what happened earlier, and asked me to give you this." I looked down and discovered that my mother's so-called gift was a tiny set of ink cartridges, the ones that went in fountain pens.

"23 ink cartridges... how useful, especially since I *totally* have a fountain pen," I said sarcastically.

"Don't think of it in a bad way," Rajesh said.

"Uh... what's the positive?"

"She wanted you to have them... for some reason which I forgot now." I looked at them.

"I won't be using it anytime soon," I told him, glaring at him.

"Okay, well, I forgave her."

"You what?" I asked.

"Forgave our mother. She really wanted to get back on good terms, and besides, it was 7 years ago that she'd made that mistake. She feels bad now."

"Why did she make the mistake in the first place?" I asked quietly.

"She was already having problems with Dad, and after coming to know that I had anxiety, she couldn't take it anymore. She actually left because she was nervous that her and Dad's problem would cause my anxiety to reach a higher point, since, well, that was the cause."

"That makes sense," I said.

"She left without telling us, because she thought that telling us would be harder on me, but she also forgot the fact that we'd come to know anyway. She wasn't thinking straight, and she was too terrified," Rajesh explained. I sighed.

"I don't know if I can forgive her so soon. As much as she tried to help us, she didn't think about how it'd affect us. The exact reason why I assumed the worst possible scenario," I said, trembling. Rajesh seemed to understand. He smiled and said,

"I'm going to go back to the room I'm staying in." He left and I glanced down at the ink cartridges. I turned it and looked at the note my mother left me.

For my lovely dancer. Hopefully you like them. You always loved to write and do calligraphy. I placed the cartridge set in my bag. We had then gone to sleep, because we had to wake up early in the morning to head back to Santa Monica. Turns out it's *not* the best idea to drive 6 hours in the evening, because you end up reaching late at night. I smiled at the thought of forgiving my mother and then fell asleep within minutes.

We woke up at around 6:00 AM and were ready by 7:30 AM. We went over to a café and had breakfast, then began driving back to Santa Monica. This time I was seated with Alan and Vanessa in a 4 seater car, and Alan's mom drove us.

"You did really good," Alan said.

"Yeah!" Vanessa agreed.

"Thanks!" We stopped for lunch, ate something, and after a few hours, arrived at ISI. We went up to our dormitory, where Hui Ying and Chathura asked me a lot of questions. I told them everything.

"Why don't we eat in the Asia Wing common room this time?" Chathura suggested. "It's less crowded."

"Oh, they serve food there?" I asked.

"On weekends, yes."

"Okay." We walked over there, where we found many other students from the Asia Wing. I walked over to a table and selected food items. As soon as we all got our food, we found a table and began eating. A few minutes later, the door opened.

"Looks like you needed a break from the crowd," Ajith said, walking towards me. I smiled.

"Not really."

"Okay. Tired?"

"No."

"Are you in pain?"

"No..." I began getting suspicious.

"Okay, then." Ajith walked away and joined another person. I continued eating. After I was done, I went over to put my plate aside. After coming back, Hui Ying smiled at me widely.

"What?" I asked.

"He cares about you," Hui Ying said in a teasing tone. I glanced at Chathura, who was also smiling at me.

"Or that could be because those symptoms are common after doing a bunch of acrobatic stunts," I said, trying to get those two to stop smiling at me that way.

"He does," Chathura smirked. "He told me last night!!"

"Hey, don't you know that Ajith told you that because it was a secret?

You just broke his trust!" I snapped, mainly because I just needed to redirect this conversation.

"Let's just call this a day," Hui Ying suggested, deciding to end the conversation. "Besides, I don't think you'd want to talk about love that much." I laughed a little at that. Not wanting to talk about love was an understatement. I *despised* talking about it. I stopped thinking about it as we went upstairs and got some sleep before another day of classes.

Eight

"Rise and shine!" Mr. Chang's voice boomed through the loudspeaker. I gasped.

"Is he in a bad mood?" I asked.

"Nope," Hui Ying said, stretching.

"That's just how he is on Mondays," Chathura said. "OH! We've got morning announcements! They're in about 30 minutes!" We got ready quickly and made it to the auditorium for the announcements.

"First of all," Mr. Chang said. "Sports teams and dance. The Track and Field team made it to finals, and the acrobatics team made it to Nationals." He glanced at the people who were cheering and added sarcastically, "Yay." I stayed silent the whole time.

"Second of all," he added, looking agitated by the amount of cheering.

"GET TO CLASS!" Everyone hurried to their classes as Rajesh and I ran to ours.

"That was good for nothing," he muttered.

"Agreed," I answered, heading to Elective with him. We continued making French pastries and today it was macaroons. This time, it took forever to get them done, because none of us could get the baking technique correct. As soon as class was over, Rajesh and I headed over to the Asia Wing common room and sat down in complete silence. Things were still awkward from the past week, so we didn't really talk much. A boy walked over to us and said,

"Rajesh, you've got practice. Don't you dare forget it. Also, I dropped out of the team." He began to walk off until I asked,

"Practice?" Suddenly, the boy stopped walking, turned around and started walking towards me.

"Nosy much?" He grabbed my wrist and held it tight. I tried to twist it free, but his grip was just too strong.

"Back off, Chenglei," Rajesh said, angrily.

"Why should I?" Chenglei sneered. "The girl shouldn't get in the middle of others' discussions. That girl ought to be taught a lesson."

"That 'girl' is my sister," Rajesh snapped. "And you have no right to get physical with her." Chenglei smirked.

"Whatever," I said, still trying to get my wrist free. "Sorry, I shouldn't have... gotten in the middle of your discussion."

"That's right. Don't do it again," Chenglei said, letting go of my wrist. Rajesh started getting really angry. I grabbed his hand quickly.

"Don't," I whispered, knowing he was going to say something. He glared at Chenglei. He walked out of the common room and I placed my hand on my forehead. Rajesh sat there and said nothing.

"If you're curious, I joined the basketball team," Rajesh said quickly. I glanced at him.

"Since when have you been interested in basketball?" I asked.

"Since your acrobatics competition. Mother encouraged me to join a sports team, and speaking of her, have you used her ink cartridges yet?"

"How can I? I don't even have a fountain pen," I replied back, sounding a bit sassy. I instantly regretted it, but at the same time, it was quite obvious.

"She asked me to give this one to you." Rajesh gave me a case. I opened it and found a black fountain pen inside.

"Okay, I guess. I'll use them another time," I said.

"Okay." The bell rang loudly, and we walked to our next class. After an hour of science, 45 minutes of art, and another hour of PE, it was time for lunch. The acrobatics team was holding a team meeting, so I attended along with my friends.

"Krithi, hi!" Araceli shouted cheerfully. I cringed. The entire school turned to look at Araceli, as her face turned scarlet red.

"Sorry," she whispered as I joined them at a restaurant. I glared at her. If not busting her, how come we did not even talk to her about the whole framing Alan thing when we were in San Jose? Or, how did we forget? It could've been because we were too focused on the competition. I stopped glaring as I sat down.

"We are at Nationals right now!!!!!! NATIONALS!" Araceli barked as we were all taken aback by the loud yelling.

"Oh, what a big surprise. We totally didn't know since, after all, none of us were at the competition! Thanks for telling us!" Alan said, sarcastically.

"I don't need the sarcasm," Araceli snapped as she rolled her eyes. "Also," she added. "There's a new team member."

"Who?" I asked.

"Look behind you," I heard a familiar voice say. I turned around, slowly observing every little detail of our new member's face.

"You?" I gasped. I backed away slowly until Chenglei grabbed my wrist again, this time holding it even more tightly. I gasped in fear.

"Hey, let me go!" I snapped.

"Listen up, Feather-head. I hear we need to dance as... couples," Chenglei said, his grip still tight, obviously ignoring my request.

"Don't phrase it that way!" I said, trying to get my wrist loose.

"You know what I mean, Feather-head. We need to dance as couples. So," his tone turned softer, his grip more loose, and I silently hoped he wasn't doing what I thought he was going to do. "Want to dance?"

"NO!" I was two seconds away from screaming that. Thankfully, I didn't say anything. I sighed.

"I'm already with someone."

"She's with Ajith," someone said.

"Why do you want to dance with her?" Vanessa asked.

"To sabotage her?" Ajith snapped. "Everyone in the Asia Wing knows about what happened earlier today."

"How?" Chenglei asked.

"Haven't you heard of gossip?" Araceli asked rudely. "Someone probably eavesdropped on your conversation and told the other... then it soon went to everyone."

"And Rajesh explained everything to me," Ajith said.

"Oh really? Okay, I honestly don't care. All that it told me was that Rajesh is an extremely overprotective brother, and people just don't know how to keep things to themselves. Anyways, I can see you clearly want answers, so to answer your previous question, Feather-head and I got off to a bad start, so... I want to start over."

"Well, that's nice... I guess, but I am partnered with Ajith," I said. He shrugged.

"Fine. I'll just dance with Araceli then." Everyone stared at him.

"I'm with someone as well! You can't compete in Nationals unless someone else joins the team," Araceli groaned.

"Fine by me," Chenglei said. He stalked away.

"Anyways, this meeting is over," Araceli said. "Go ahead and join the rest of... whoever you plan on hanging out with." Ajith and I walked away from them and joined Rajesh and Chathura.

"Chai? We have it here." Rajesh offered me a cup of the spiced tea.

"Sure." I took the cup and sipped slowly. "Wow!"

"I know, right?" Rajesh said. "It transports us back home."

"To Atlantic City? No-" I began.

"No, not Atlantic City. Amaravati. Where we first lived."

"You're right," I said, instantly making the connection. "Mom used to make it every time we came back from our school in India."

"Her tea was the best," Rajesh remarked. "I always liked how she added a clove in it."

"I know, right? This one seems to be missing a clove," I pointed out.

"Excuse me, I'm loving the conversation here, but, uh, *we* exist too," Chathura interrupted.

"Oh, sorry," I said. Chathura smirked in response.

"Can't you give those two a break?" Ajith asked. Chathura rolled her eyes at him.

"I never give breaks," she responded.

"JUST GIVE UP FOR ONCE!" Ajith screamed. I covered my mouth in shock, Chathura smirked, and Rajesh stared at Ajith, his eyes filled with worry. Ajith closed his eyes and put his hands on his forehead, sighing. I could see that he didn't want to be questioned about it, so I finished my tea and I sat there listening to Chathura tease Rajesh about... who knows what.

"So," Ajith said, startling me. I looked at him. He looked a lot less angry now.

"So... what?" I asked.

"Um... there's a dance coming up. *A school dance.*" I kept quiet as Ajith stared straight ahead.

"Do you... maybe want to go together?" He asked after a couple of seconds. Chathura gave one final insult, then stared at us. Rajesh looked at me in complete shock. Chathura smiled.

"Go for it," she said. "Besides, I want to see my brother fool himself on the dance floor!" Ajith glared at her.

"To be quite fair, I am a pretty average dancer." I looked at my friends and nodded.

"Okay... yes. I'll go with you," I finally agreed. Ajith smiled.

"I'm so glad. Ajith isn't ready for rejection... especially from the love of his life," Chathura told us. Ajith and I glared at her at the same time.

"Oh? Then you'd better prepare him for it," Chenglei's voice appeared from behind us. I rolled my eyes.

"Why don't you take your own advice, Chenglei? Stop eavesdropping on us," Rajesh snapped. He walked over to me, grabbed my wrist and held it tightly for the third time, and said,

"Oh, I'm not eavesdropping anymore, am I? I already eavesdropped, and *I* want to take Feather-head out to the dance."

Nine

"Okay, you're asking me to dance, *why*?!"

"I like you," Chenglei said. It was as simple as that. He said the words and didn't blush or anything. I eyed him suspiciously. Most people blush if they admit their feelings to girls, so was this actually true?

"Ugh, if you like her so much then why do you call her Feather-head?" Chathura asked.

"Because her personality is quite soft." I looked at him in confusion. *Soft*?

"Sorry to disappoint you," Rajesh said. "Krithi's already going out with someone."

"You always state the obvious, Rajesh," Chenglei sneered. "Oh and that's your name? I was going to continue calling you Feather-head."

"Yeah, I'd much prefer my real name over... that," I said.

"Okay, who are you going out with?"

"Him," Rajesh gestured to Ajith.

"Fine, let's bet," Chenglei said to Ajith, while the latter shook his head.

"No, no, NO! That's not necessary! Please don't bet!" I said.

"Chenglei are you out of your mind?" Rajesh yelled.

"No. Let's bet," Chenglei said, rudely.

"That isn't necessary!" I repeated. "It's just a stupid dance. If you guys bet on it, I'm not going with either of you!" Chenglei glared at me, Ajith seemed to have had the same thoughts about betting as I did, Rajesh looked anxious again, and Chathura was clapping the whole time. I glared at her, and she shrugged. I continued glaring at Chenglei until he finally gave up.

"Fine, take... that guy to the dance."

"His name is *Ajith*," I said.

"Whatever. I will date you one day," Chenglei stalked off. I lightly facepalmed.

"I'm sorry," I said to Ajith later.

"Hey, don't worry about it. I've known Chenglei since I attended this school. I've been his rival for a long time," Ajith informed me.

"Really?" I asked.

"Definitely," Ajith assured me. "I made the basketball team last year. He didn't. He made it this year. I decided not to try out."

"And he was happy about that, I assume," I guessed.

"Yeah." We packed up and headed to our next class, and just like that, our day went by quickly.

"Focus!" Mrs. Sayuri said, as we practiced our routines later that day in acrobatics. "We made it to Nationals, but that's not enough. We have to beat Félicité!" I sighed.

"I wish we weren't focusing on beating a certain team," Ajith said.

"I know," I replied. "More like in this case, it's a certain person. It looks as if my previous dance teacher and Mrs. Sayuri are serious rivals." He nodded and we decided to practice our routine. I failed the throw and catch, like usual.

"Try the move we did during our routine at the competition. It might be a little easier." I got into a perfect position on Ajith's hands, attempted the move, and fell again. I frowned. I'm usually able to do it!

"What am I doing wrong?" I wondered out loud.

"Don't try anymore. You could hurt yourself," Ajith said. A few minutes later, acrobatics ended and we went to go change. After we changed back into our uniforms, we met at the food court along with Rajesh and Chathura. As soon as we got our food, we walked over to a table and began eating.

"How was basketball?" Chathura asked Rajesh.

"Fine," Rajesh replied. "It was... different without Chenglei."

"How?" I asked.

"He's our star player. We have a game against a team in the higher leagues in a few months. We don't stand a chance without him," he explained. "Don't you dare tell him I said that," he added to us.

"Why would we?" I asked.

"Yeah, and besides, that's months away," Chathura said. "Don't worry about it." Rajesh glared at Chathura. I smiled a little.

"Leave it to them to start the worst relationship in the whole school," Ajith said. "They're complete opposites! Rajesh is shy... no offense," he added when he saw Rajesh raising his eyebrows. "He spends a lot of time alone or with just Krithi... he's kind hearted and always makes sure his friends and family are okay, while my sister is-"

"Straightforward and arrogant. I guess if it's my friends or family, I'll make sure they're okay, *only* if they look upset, as in *really* upset,"

Chathura interrupted. "Oh, and don't forget my amazing teasing! There's no way *that's* stopping." I stared at Chathura for a couple of seconds. She shrugged.

"Yes, that is her personality," Ajith said.

"How about you two?" I asked.

"How similar would you say you are?" Rajesh asked.

"You name our personality traits and see for yourself," Chathura said.

"Well, Chathura is... what she said she is. Ajith is... Krithi, you know him a bit better. You can define his traits." I thought about it for a couple seconds, then said,

"He is kind, thinks before he speaks, and he's a little quiet, but not necessarily shy. He can be disorganized at times-"

"Hey!" Ajith interrupted, glaring at me. "I'm *not* disorganized."

"Whatever. Okay, well, uh... he's good at making connections-"

"Wow, you really don't know me well enough," Ajith said as he rolled his eyes.

"Leave it to the professionals," Chathura smirked. "Ajith is kind, very organized... for everything besides acrobatics. He makes lists, tables, and charts for many things. He was born very uptight and disciplined. I was born carefree and laid back. I think you know the rest of the traits."

"Wow," Rajesh said. "Well... um... change of subject. When are the Nationals?"

"In about 6 weeks. Mrs. Sayuri said we should be extra careful. We can't result in any injuries now," I told him.

"Wow... then there's Worlds," Ajith said. "We never made it to Worlds."

"We can... this time... I hope," I said. I knew it might be impossible.

"Have you ever made it to worlds when you were on Félicité's team?" Chathura asked.

"No," I said. "We've made it to Nationals before, but not any further. Worlds are probably next to impossible."

"Well, after the way Ajith and Krithi danced together, it might be possible," Rajesh said. "But in order to beat Félicité's team, you'll have to do something more... advanced."

"I tried," I admitted. "I kept failing at it."

"What skill did you try out?"

"A throw and catch move."

"It's really difficult and scary," Ajith said. "Krithi's been practicing since we first met."

"Let me guess. You stared into each others' eyes as she did whatever it is she did, your eyes glowing with love?" Chathura teased. I glared at her. So did Ajith and Rajesh. We all seemed to be having the same question in mind. I decided to ask it.

"Does she ever shut up?" I asked.

"No," Ajith said. "It was the same with... never mind."

"Who?" I asked.

"No one," Ajith replied, embarrassment reflected on his face.

"You can tell us," Rajesh assured him.

"I'll gladly spill it," Chathura volunteered.

"NO!" We three yelled at the same time.

"Hey, I volunteered. There's no way Ajith's going to tell you. Take it or leave it," Chathura shrugged. Ajith rolled his eyes.

"Fine, before my sister explains the most embarrassing moment of my life, I should do it myself. I used to like this girl when I was 7. We were obviously too young to date, and Chathura eventually found out... and I couldn't lie. Chathura and the girl were close friends and she busted me. I was mad at her for weeks, until our father told us to make up."

"We did. I said I was sorry I told the girl about it, and he said he was sorry he got angry," Chathura said.

"Oh and by the way, you might know her. She moved to Atlantic City and she loves acrobatics," Ajith said.

"Who is it?" I asked. Ajith looked at Chathura, then said,

"Some girl called Asheni."

"Asheni... as in Asheni Kumara?" I gasped.

"Yes," Chathura said.

"She and her sister Anuradha were my only friends in the acrobatics team," I said.

"Yeah, Asheni was my best friend until the whole busting Ajith thing," Chathura said. "And Anuradha knows me too."

"Asheni mentioned you," I suddenly remembered.

"Who, me?" Ajith and Chathura said at the same time. They stared at each other, and Chathura shrugged.

"Ajith," I said. "I just didn't think it was the same one."

"Really? What did she say about me?" Ajith asked.

"She said you were kind and she did like you, but she doesn't exactly have a crush on you anymore. She has a new one."

"Who?" Chathura asked.

"That's personal," I said. "I don't think she wants anyone to know."

"Fair enough," Chathura agreed, shrugging again. "Anyways, if we're done spilling life stories, we can head to the Asia Wing common room. Though I've always been interested in why Rajesh is so overprotective of Krithi."

"Yeah, change of topic," Ajith said quickly.

"No, it's fine," Rajesh and I both said at the same time.

"The reason he's overprotective of me is because, when I had depression, people took that opportunity to make fun of me and do awful things, and Rajesh is just trying to make sure it doesn't happen again," I explained. Rajesh nodded.

"Oh, okay. What happened, though?" Ajith asked.

"I... don't really want to explain," I said.

"That's fair," he told me. We began walking to the Asia Wing common room, then I stopped.

"What's up?" Ajith asked.

"Um... Ajith, do they keep the gymnasium open after practice?" I asked.

"Yeah... why?"

"I... think I should practice a little more."

"I can go with you," Ajith offered.

"Okay," I said. As Chathura and Rajesh headed towards the Asia Wing common room, Ajith and I started walking towards the gymnasium and found Mrs. Sayuri there.

"Hi!" Mrs. Sayuri said. "Did you want to practice?"

"Yeah," I said. We got into a starting position and got ready to attempt the throw and catch. Naturally, I fell again.

"Okay, why don't we stick with what you can actually do," Ajith suggested. I got into the starting position, completed the front flips all the way down, but then I fell for some reason, and I heard a loud scream. I gasped as I saw Ajith clutching his ankle, screaming in pain.

Ten

"What happened?" I asked, staring at Ajith in concern. He was screaming in pain and tears were rolling down his face.

"He hurt himself," Mrs. Sayuri explained. "His ankle rolled as he fell while he tried to hoist you back up again. We have to get him to the hospital." She ran over to Mr. Chang's office to tell him what happened. I walked over, knelt beside him, and put my hand on his shoulder which was jerking in all sorts of directions. It stopped as soon as my hand made contact with it, which somehow managed to calm him down.

"Try to divert your mind elsewhere," I advised, but immediately wished I hadn't, because there's no way that someone could *divert their mind elsewhere* when they're in that much pain. He did as he was told, though, and his screaming subsided a little.

"Mr. Chang said that we can drive him to a hospital," Mrs. Sayuri informed me, running inside the gym.

"I'll help," I offered, slinging his arm around my shoulders. I slung Ajith's other arm around Mrs. Sayuri's shoulders and we both helped get him over to Mrs. Sayuri's car, and we drove over to the hospital. We carried him inside and we were provided with a wheelchair. A doctor soon came inside the room we were instructed to go to, and asked, "What happened?"

"He twisted his ankle badly... I think," Mrs. Sayuri said. We helped Ajith lay down on a cot and the doctor placed his leg on an elevated platform.

"I'll do a quick X-ray," the doctor said. She removed Ajith's leg from the platform, brought a device in, and instructed him to place his leg in many different directions. I couldn't imagine how it could've been for him, but he was very calm... or he pretended to be. After a few minutes the X-ray came in.

"Okay, don't freak out," the doctor said. "He's sprained his ankle."

"What?!" Mrs. Sayuri and I yelled at the same time.

"Yes. It's okay, though. It is a minor one, though we aren't sure if he can participate in that competition of yours," the doctor said.

"Oh no," Mrs. Sayuri said. "Okay. That's okay. I understand. Thanks Taylor." Taylor, which was apparently the doctor's name, left the room. I sat down on a chair next to Ajith.

"Krithi, I am so sorry," he apologized. "I should've been more careful."

"No, do not blame yourself," I said as I took his hand. "It's not your fault. If anything, it's mine."

"No, that's not true. What makes you think that?"

"I must've done too many flips just like I did during the competition. You wouldn't have hurt yourself if I was careful."

"Don't say that, Krithi. You did an adequate amount of flips. Something must've happened while I tried to hoist you, that's all," Ajith reassured me. I smiled nervously.

"Are you okay?" Mrs. Sayuri asked, breaking our conversation.

"No. Definitely not," Ajith replied. Taylor returned with a brace for Ajith's leg, and carefully fit it on him.

"Here, use these," Taylor gave Ajith crutches.

"Thanks," Ajith said. He got up, we drove back to the school, and we helped him get to the Asia Wing common room. Mrs. Sayuri walked back to the studio, and I filled a cup of water and gave it to him. He drank it and thanked me. We sat down and I stared at his brace. I must've looked lost in thought, because Ajith asked,

"Are you okay?"

"Yeah, just fine."

"You know you might have to dance with Chenglei, right?" I thought about that for a couple of seconds and said,

"Yeah… but that's not a big deal."

"Seriously?"

"What can be done now? You sprained your ankle, and there's a possibility that you can't compete."

"You're positive?"

"Yes. I am," I said. "Let's just hope he doesn't use this as his chance to flirt with me."

"Right," Ajith said.

"I forgot that my brother has competition," Chathura said, who was apparently eavesdropping on that one part of the conversation. How was she always there whenever something about love comes up?!

"Just shut up," Ajith snapped.

"Not happening," Chathura said, this time in a more teasing way. It was right at that moment when she noticed Ajith's ankle brace. "Oh my gosh, what happened?!"

"I sprained my ankle."

"Are you okay?!"

"Yeah, I'm fine."

"Seriously?!" Chathura gasped.

"Chathura, it's alright. I'm fine." She covered her eyes in shock.

"Chathura, are *you* okay?" I asked as her expression turned from shock to worry.

"Yeah, I'm fine," she said. "We should get to bed now." We agreed and Ajith went in a separate direction while Chathura and I went one way. We finally made it back to our dormitory and fell asleep within seconds.

"You've got this, everyone. Keep focusing on your tumbling moves!" Mrs. Sayuri seemed extra encouraging today. Right after helping someone, she approached me.

"Hey, Krithi?"

"Yeah?" I asked.

"Do you want to dance with Chenglei? I figured since you don't have a partner-"

"I will," I said, flatly. Mrs. Sayuri shrugged and walked away.

"Where's Ajith?" Alan asked.

"Sprained ankle. He's in his dormitory right now."

"I'm sorry that happened to him. Tell him I hope he feels better. Hey, why don't you dance with-"

"I will," I said, knowing exactly what he was going to say. He shrugged, turned around and gasped at... who knows what.

"What is it?" I asked.

"Look behind you," Sienna said. I turned around and gasped. Chenglei was warming up, and he performed a double twist and landed it perfectly.

"You should probably work with him to get your throw and catch correct," Sienna suggested.

"I will," I said for the third time, and walked over to him and he finished his perfect warm up.

"So," Chenglei said. "You finally want to date?"

"No!" I snapped.

"Okay. Well, why are you here? No offense."

"I just saw your double twist, and it looked really good. I mean, I've never seen such a good one," I said.

"Really? Well, I'm flattered, but what are you *really* doing here?"

"Ugh, fine. I am supposed to dance with you since Ajith may not be able to compete," I said, flatly. "And I need help on a throw and catch move." I explained the move to him and he said,

"I don't need to help you. You already can do it."

"No, I can't. You know well enough that I fail at it every time," I said, annoyed. I had no idea what Chenglei's angle was, but I had no intention of finding out. I just wanted him to stop with his fake enthusiasm or whatever it was.

"You can do it! The only thing you need is confidence... and practice," he eventually said, which jerked me out of my thoughts. I rolled my eyes.

"Ugh whatever. You haven't been any help whatsoever." I stalked off to another area to practice, and caught Ajith and Rajesh staring through the window. I gave them a confused look as I practiced single front tucks. As soon as acrobatics was over, I went to a changing room, changed into my uniform, and walked over to both of them and asked, "What are you two doing?!"

"Well, I kind of wanted to see how things were going and Rajesh was already here. It looks like you're talking to Chenglei," Ajith said.

"Yeah. Is he bothering you?" Rajesh asked.

"No. We're partners now," I said. "My only option," I added when I saw Rajesh's eyebrows shoot up.

"That's good," Ajith said, smiling.

"Yeah," I said. I grabbed my bag and stuffed my water bottle inside, and we made our way over to the food court. As soon as we sat down at an open table, they stared at me, concerned.

"Are you okay?" Ajith asked.

"Yeah, I'm fine," I lied. "Wait, where's Chathura?"

"Hey guys, did you miss me? Sorry. Extracurriculars took over," Chathura's voice suddenly appeared out of nowhere. She walked over and slammed her hands on the table. She then sat next to Rajesh.

"So, about that dance. Who all are going?"

"I might," Rajesh said.

"I don't know if I will," I said.

"Oh come on, just because your little boyfriend isn't going, doesn't mean you should miss out on it!" Chathura exclaimed. I covered my eyes to hide my blush.

"Chathura, just because I asked her out to the dance, that does not automatically make us a couple!" Ajith groaned. "AND I AM NOT LITTLE!"

"You're forgetting that I'm 16.5 minutes older than you," Chathura smirked. Ajith facepalmed and said,

"How *could* I forget? You remind me so often."

"Who's younger out of you and Krithi?" Chathura asked Rajesh.

"I'm older by eight minutes," Rajesh said.

"Oh nice," Ajith said.

"Now can we change the topic?" I asked.

"Okay, so back to the dance," Chathura said. "The point is, if Ajith doesn't go, that doesn't mean you shouldn't."

"Well, the thing is, I wouldn't have gone unless I was asked by someone," I explained. "I generally hate these events and if I was asked to go, I actually had a reason."

"Okay," Chathura said.

"Are you going with anyone?" Rajesh asked her.

"You're trying to ask me to go with you, aren't you?" Chathura responded, smirking. Ajith and I stared at her in confusion. I raised my eyebrows at her.

"It's either I've got the best intuition out of all of us, or Rajesh makes it super obvious. Probably the latter, but maybe the first," she continued. Ajith rolled his eyes.

"It's either my sister embarrasses someone by saying no, or she has an excuse to overpraise herself right after saying yes. Both are to her advantage," he murmured.

"Oh, don't feel bad, little brother. I'm sure you'll catch up," Chathura sneered.

"I'm *not* little," Ajith repeated. "You were only born a *few* minutes before me."

"Again, it was 16.5," Chathura shot back. "Also, what about Krithi and Rajesh? They both are probably older than us, right? That classifies you as Krithi's *little boyfriend.*"

"Our birthday is on December 3rd," I said.

"And ours is on October 12th," Ajith said, smiling at Chathura as she rolled her eyes.

"Ugh, fine, whatever." That was the first time we'd finally beat Chathura at her own game. I smiled as well.

"So, get to the point. Are you trying to ask me to the dance?" Chathura asked Rajesh.

"I- maybe," Rajesh answered shyly.

"You should totally ask!" Ajith encouraged him.

"You both will have a great time," I added.

"Okay, I will," Rajesh told us, smiling a little.

"I'm waiting," Chathura said. Rajesh stayed silent for a couple seconds.

"*Still* waiting!" Chathura pressed.

"Okay, okay! Be patient," Rajesh snapped back.

"For the record, this is *not* the correct way to ask anyone-" Ajith began, but was soon interrupted by Chathura, who snapped back,

"Oh shut up, little brother and let Rajesh ask." Ajith facepalmed again and sighed. He looked over at me, and I shrugged.

"Chathura... would you like to go to the dance together?" Rajesh asked, looking at his hands on his lap.

"I would, but I need a more *sincere* request," Chathura said. I raised my eyebrows at her. Rajesh sighed.

"Chathura, do you want to go to the dance together," he said a little less timidly.

"Why, I would love to," Chathura answered, smiling. Rajesh returned it nervously.

"Congratulations!" I said.

"Oh come on, it's not like he's proposing, you don't have to congratulate us," Chathura said.

"Uh..." I said. "Isn't that something everyone says for good things?"

"Yeah. I guess so," Chathura shrugged. "Seriously, make it quicker next time," she added in a serious tone to Rajesh.

"Now I'm wondering *why* I asked her in the first place," Rajesh muttered.

"Because I'm beautiful, amazing, and just cannot be resisted," Chathura answered. Ajith facepalmed for the third time and I grabbed his hand and said,

"Don't."

"So, what dress will you wear?" Chathura asked.

"Again, I am unsure if I'm going," I said.

"Okay, well at least make your brother go tuxedo shopping." Rajesh glared at her.

"I already *have* a tuxedo." Those two broke into an argument about that and I shook my head and rolled my eyes.

"Why did Rajesh ask my sister?" Ajith asked me.

"I have no idea. Honestly, he likes who he likes, and we aren't one to judge," I whispered to him.

"Seriously, though, he likes Chathura, that's not a big deal," Ajith said.

"What's your point?" I asked. Ajith hesitated and said,

"Does Chathura even like him back?"

Eleven

What I wanted to say was,

"Probably." I knew Rajesh would feel like he's a fool if he'd asked someone and found out later that they were faking it. I didn't want to make any snap judgments, but I didn't want to lie either.

"Maybe," I eventually said, eyeing Chathura, who looked pleased with the whole relationship. "She looks pleased, so maybe we shouldn't worry too much about it."

"I agree," Ajith said. It was just at that moment when I spotted a pair of crutches and remembered that they were Ajith's.

"How's your ankle, by the way?" I asked.

"I'm in a bit of pain, but it should stop hurting soon," Ajith said. He tried to put up a front about it, but I could tell he was secretly very angry. I decided not to talk to him about it. Instead I just watched Chathura and Rajesh argue.

"They have a very interesting relationship," I pointed out, changing the subject. I turned to Ajith, but he wasn't there. I glanced over at Chathura and Rajesh and asked,

"Do both of you know where Ajith is?"

"No idea," Rajesh said.

"I don't know, but maybe he went to the gymnasium," Chathura said. Rajesh and I stared at her.

"Why would he be in the gymnasium?!" I asked. "He's sprained his ankle!"

"Well, maybe he's just... there," Chathura suggested. "He loves acrobatics, and any time he's upset, he'd go over to the gymnasium and stay there... but he might be anywhere else, since, well... he sprained his ankle, but I'll assume he's in the gymnasium asking Ms. Sayuri about some of the upcoming competitions." I nodded and said,

"Okay, I'm going to go check."

"We're coming too," Chathura and Rajesh both said simultaneously. They immediately glared at each other and Chathrura blushed. I rolled my eyes at them. We went over to the gymnasium to find Ajith speaking to Mrs. Sayuri. Mrs. Sayuri was nodding, while Ajith seemed to have been speaking very seriously. Ajith caught sight of us and rolled his eyes.

"Sorry," Chathura whispered to him guiltily.

"So, what's your reason for spying on me?" Ajith asked curtly. Mrs. Sayuri's face turned pale.

"I'm going to get out of here," she said, then headed off in a hurry. She probably sensed a bad argument forming, and I hoped that her senses were wrong. As soon as she left, Ajith glared at all of us.

"We aren't *spying* on you," Chathura said sheepishly, but Ajith did not buy it for one second.

"It clearly looks like you were," he replied, arrogantly.

"We wanted to make sure you are okay," I reasoned with him gently.

"Yeah. You're our friend and we are really worried about you," Rajesh added.

"I'm fine," Ajith sighed. "Seriously, I am."

"That's what most people say when they're upset," Rajesh and Chathura said simultaneously again. They stared at each other and Chathura blushed again.

"Okay, we *really* need to quit saying things at the same time," she said. Ajith laughed a little at that.

"Anyways. Most people say they're fine, when they're really not," Chathura explained. "And I can tell that you're faking, since well, you're my brother."

"Any time Krithi is upset, she tries to hide it. There are rare times when she actually tells me what happened, because she's afraid of admitting the truth," Rajesh added. I widened my eyes at him, deeply embarrassed.

"Why are you telling him this?!" I asked, raising my eyebrows.

"Sorry," Rajesh said. "I didn't mean to tell him anything personal. I was just trying to use an example."

"Okay then," I said, feeling a little less embarrassed.

"Well, I'm not covering anything up," Ajith said, but he looked at Chathura a little guiltily, who whispered,

"Liar." She glared at Ajith in a way I've never seen before. Ajith placed his fingertips on his forehead and turned away. He inhaled deeply and stared ahead.

"Are you okay?" Rajesh asked, though I was unsure who he was directing it to.

"You are a liar!" Chathura screamed again at Ajith. That was the most angry I've ever seen her get.

"Hey, calm down! What happened?" I asked, grabbing her hand. I've never seen her like this. She ignored me and continued yelling.

"You remember what happened when I broke my ankle, right?! Remember what happened to me?" Oddly, this story seemed a little familiar, but different at the same time.

"Chathura, please. I promise, everything will be better if you just calm down," Rajesh advised her, but she ignored him as well. Ajith stared at her, feeling even more guilty with every word.

"You remember it well enough, Ajith! I've been keeping my cool this whole time, but you didn't even think to speak to me about what's bothering you. Well, guess what? I know what's bothering you. You don't like being on crutches, and you hate the fact that you're hurt in the first place! Now you're keeping your anger inside, and soon you'll offend the people you love!" Chathura was two seconds away from crying. "I made the same mistake and then... well... you know what happened," she added. Ajith continued staring at her, but this one was more like a glare. He didn't seem so guilty anymore.

"Just because you were sent to live in a boarding school since you lacked discipline and respect, does not mean I will. Unlike you, I am tame and don't need to learn anything," he snapped and left the studio. Chathura ran and ran in the other direction. Rajesh and I ran after her until we found ourselves in the Asia Wing common room. Chathura was sobbing on a couch and Rajesh and I walked over. We were alone in the Asia Wing common room for some reason today, which was actually a good thing now that I thought about it, since no one will question Chathura.

"Are you okay?" I asked, then immediately regretted saying it. I expected an arrogant remark from her, but instead, she just shook her head. I sat down next to her, and Rajesh did the same on the other side. We wrapped our arms around her shoulders as she sobbed.

"You'll be okay," I whispered soothingly. "You're an amazing person and you've made so many accomplishments." Rajesh used to use that technique on me, so I tried it out. Rajesh raised his eyebrows at me and I shrugged.

"I won't be. It's been haunting me since I was 8," Chathura muttered.

"What is it?" Rajesh asked, gently.

"When I was living in Sri Lanka, I wasn't who I was now," she said.

"Then what were you?" I asked.

"I was a kind, caring, and beautiful child," she said. "I had a great life there, my parents loved me, and everything. That's when I broke my ankle when I was 8 years old. I knew my parents were already dealing with a lot, considering my father got fired from his job and we were supposed to move to Santa Monica for a new job, so I kept my anger inside. Eventually, I couldn't do it anymore. I burst on my parents. I yelled at them and Ajith. Ajith was scared, my parents would've been scared, but the loss of my dad's job made both of their personalities change from fragile and delicate, to hard and rigid. They thought I was being extremely disrespectful, and warned me to stop. I *couldn't* stop, though. I'd tested their patience so much that they'd threatened to send me to another place and have me live there. I didn't think they were going to actually go with it, but they did. They told me to pack my bags the next day, and sent me to a horribly strict boarding school... which I forgot the location of. The last thing that I saw of my family that day was Ajith's scared face. I lived there for 5 years, and my cousin lived there too, and he was amazing and kind. He understood why I burst on my parents and told me that everyone makes mistakes. When I was 13 years old, he said that I should move to Santa Monica. There was a great school there and I should be with my brother. I left on a flight by myself and met my parents there, who were waiting at the airport. They seemed to have welcomed me, but that only lasted for a day. Soon, they went back to their rigid selves... or at least my mom did. My dad became a better person, regrets his actions, and we got back on good terms."

"That's awful," I said, after Chathura finished her story.

"I'm so sorry," Rajesh said. "And what you first said isn't true at all. You *are* kind and caring."

"And very pretty," I added, rubbing her back.

"Thank you. Anyways, I was really worried about Ajith, so I exploded. Nothing like what happened to me would've ever happened to him, but still, I didn't want him to make the same mistake I did," Chathura said.

"That makes sense," I whispered. I got up, poured her a cup of water, and handed it to her. She drank a little, and fresh tears started rolling down her cheeks.

"We should talk to Ajith," Rajesh suggested.

"He won't listen to you," Chathura replied. "He's right now in a really bad mood." As soon as the words were said, someone came into the common room. I turned back to see Ajith staring at Chathura, who rolled her eyes. Ajith moved towards us and stood in front of Chathura.

"Save it Ajith," she snapped. She glared at him so hard, I wondered if her eyes hurt.

"Look, I'm sorry. I didn't mean to-" Ajith began but Chathura started crying again. I looked up at him and sighed.

"It wasn't as easy as you thought," I said gently. "It was hard for her."

"I- I always thought that our parents selected a good school for her-" Ajith tried to speak again, but this time, Chathura stopped him mid-sentence.

"Well, they didn't. This boarding school didn't even teach proper school subjects. I had to study on my own. You know what we learned? Decorum, etiquette, that kind of stuff," Chathura said, harshly. "It's almost as if I was sent to a reform school to learn good behavior rather than an actual school itself."

"How were our parents supposed to know that?!" Ajith snapped back.

"They didn't," Chathura admitted. "I told them. Mom didn't care, but Dad did." Ajith took a couple of deep breaths to refrain from yelling at her and sighed.

"Okay... I'm sorry, I didn't know," he said. "And I guess you have a point... with what you said earlier, and I'm so sorry for what I said."

"It's fine," Chathura said, drying her eyes. "I'm sorry for blowing up at you in the first place, but please tell me, were you angry about your ankle at all?"

"Not necessarily *angry*," Ajith admitted. "Just... impatient."

"Oh," Chathura, Rajesh, and I said simultaneously. We weren't exactly expecting that. We looked at each other, then back at Ajith.
"Um... it's getting late," I said to break the silence.
"Yeah, we should go," Rajesh said. We left the Asia Wing common room and went to our dormitories. There, after a long and exhausting day, everything seemed better.

Twelve

Time flew by and before I knew it, the weekend arrived. Rajesh and I decided to head home for a couple days rather than stay at the school for the weekend, because it had been an eventful week and we wanted a bit of time by ourselves. Ajith and Chathura did the same, and I assumed they felt the same way.

"Hey Krithi," Rajesh said from behind me.

"Hi," I said. "Dad should be here."

"Relax, he's coming," Rajesh replied. "Wait... are you okay?"

"Yeah, I'm fine," I said, and actually meant it.

"Are you sure?" Rajesh asked. "You seem anxious."

"I promise, I'm fine," I assured him.

"Wait," I said, looking at his facial expression, which seemed as if he was agitated and angry at the same time. "Are *you* okay?"

"Fine," he lied. He looked as if he didn't want to speak about it, so I didn't say a thing. We stood there in complete silence until Dad and Christina walked into the school. We walked down to meet them and I held back from screaming as Christina squeezed me hard.

"Hi, Christina... you can let go of me now," I said. Christina released me quickly.

"Sorry. I just missed you SO MUCH." Okay, this was not like Christina. The way she was acting was way too annoying... though her usual self was also annoying. Besides, it's not like she was actually my mother! How did she miss me *already*?!

"Are... you okay?" I whispered to her.

"Yes, yes! I'm *just* fine!!!" Christina said, eagerly. Rajesh and I gave her concerned looks, but figured she didn't want to admit what was upsetting her so we didn't bother to ask. We walked over to the car and Dad and Christina spoke for a long time while we headed home. As soon as we headed home, I observed the details of the house again... until I saw Rajesh staring straight ahead.

"What are you looking at?" I asked.

"Krithi, Rajesh!" A horribly familiar voice exclaimed. I gasped and turned to stand face to face with my mother. *Again*!

"Mom?" I asked. "I thought you went back to India."

"I decided to stay for a little longer."

"Okay," I responded.

"Why don't you both... do something. Your father, *Crystal*, and I need to discuss something."

"My name is *Christina*, not *Crystal*," I overheard Christina growl as I walked towards the gymnasium. I walked inside, warmed up, and dragged out an inclined mat. I practiced single front tucks first, then successfully performed a double front tuck. I practiced a few other moves until Rajesh walked in.

"This looks really nice," he said. "I've never been here before." I smiled and nodded. He watched carefully as I tried to do a double twist after a round off and a back handspring. I fell and I got back up.

"Are you sure you are okay?" Rajesh asked again. I frowned as I turned around to face him and said,

"I'm fine, and I've told you that over and over again! Can you stop asking me that?" Rajesh stayed silent for a couple seconds, then he looked at me angrily.

"If this is about Mom, I told you, it was nothing! Why are you holding a grudge? She did nothing to you! You should seriously get over it," he snapped back. That was the first time he fought back in any sort of argument between us both. We barely argue, though.

"It's not as easy as you think!" I screamed, extremely aggravated.

"You think I don't know that?! Well, I'm the reason she left! It may have been for a good cause but I am *still* the reason!" Rajesh yelled back. "You don't think I know how hard it is?!"

"Both of you, what is going on here?!" Christina opened the door.

"Nothing," I said quickly.

"Well, Aishwarya is nervous. This 'yelling' is making her wonder if you both are okay," Christina said, using my mother's first name.

"We're fine," Rajesh said. I nodded and got off the inclined mat. I got into a starting position for the double twist again and Rajesh gasped.

"Stop! Don't do it!" I ignored him and attempted the double twist after a round off and back handspring... and used too much power in the twist to accidentally go into a third twist, but not enough to land it. I fell and landed on my side, and I immediately wished I had set up a mat underneath. I screamed as pain seared through me, and I heard fast footsteps. Rajesh kneeled beside me and tried to help me get up. I felt really overwhelmed with the crowd, so I stayed still.

"Krithi, you should try getting up," Dad said.

"Please," my mother added. "I promise, you will be fine." My parents obviously thought that I was in immense pain, but now that I thought about it, I wasn't in much pain... not anymore, at least. I finally got up and Rajesh and Christina helped me walk to my room. Christina helped me get into my bed and I sat down with the pillows set up in a straight position to help me sit properly. Rajesh sat down on the edge of the bed and stared at the walls while I stared ahead. I could tell he felt really uncomfortable and nervous. I couldn't blame him.

"I'm sorry," I said. "I blew up on you and I really shouldn't have."

"What happened?" Rajesh asked. "You rarely blow up like that!"

"I- well... I don't know if I can say." Rajesh stayed silent for a few seconds.

"You can tell me," he eventually said.

"Well, Ajith's sprained ankle has kind of been bothering me," I admitted. "It was scary to see him in so much pain after he fell." I expected Rajesh to call me crazy or something, but he instead said,

"I understand." That was the thing I really admired about him. He was able to understand just about anything.

"Krithi, are you okay?" My mother walked into the room and looked at me, concerned.

"Fine," I said, staring at Rajesh, who looked away. He placed his fingertips on his forehead, and shook his head in annoyance.

"Okay, well I'm going somewhere else," he said quietly and left.

"I know you're angry at me," Mom whispered. "And I understand, but I hope Rajesh told you what I told him."

"He did," I said. "And I'm not angry at you for the reason anymore. I am still angry that you left in the first place, though."

"What did Indumathi tell you?" Mom sighed.

"Indumathi as in our *maid*?"

"You tell me. Do we know anyone else called Indumathi?"

"No..." I said. "Well, Indumathi told Rajesh that you didn't like Dad, so you left. Three days later, she pulled *me* aside and said that you left because of Rajesh's anxiety and told me not to tell Rajesh."

"Guess all three of you took it the wrong way," Mom said.

"Yeah, well, Rajesh told me everything after the acrobatics competition, so, I know. It's just... it hasn't been easy living without you, especially because I don't get to see you."

"I know, but things haven't gone well between me and your dad. I haven't been completely honest with your brother either."

"What do you mean?" I asked.

"Why don't I get your brother and I'll explain everything." My mother began to walk out of the room, but then paused.

"Are you in pain?" she asked, turning towards me.

"I'm feeling much better, thank you." My mother smiled (a real one, not one of her artificial ones she pulled off at the competition) and left. I managed to sit up, and a few seconds later, she came back with Rajesh. They both sat down on my bed and my mother sighed.

"I haven't been honest with you both. Krithi, Indumathi had you believing that I left because I was too embarrassed to be around Rajesh. Rajesh, I told you that I tried to help you. Those two reasons weren't... exactly the truth."

"What's the truth then?" I asked.

"It's... I'm too embarrassed to admit that I left for this reason." I looked at my mother and realized she was crying. That was the first time I'd ever seen her cry. I covered my mouth in shock and sympathy. Rajesh put his hand on her arm and rubbed it, attempting to comfort her.

"Everyone makes mistakes," I whispered. "I made a massive one a couple of weeks ago."

"Yeah, and I've made plenty before," Rajesh whispered. "You can tell us. We won't get mad at you."

"Okay... fine. Well, the reason I left was... I was afraid," Mom explained, slowly. "I wasn't afraid of harming anyone... I was just... scared."

"What were you afraid of?" I asked.

"My sister Lavanya was diagnosed with anxiety... and it was a hard thing for my family. My brothers and other sisters stayed away from her, and she started to feel even more miserable. I wished that didn't happen to her. When I found out that Rajesh had anxiety, I tried to remain calm at that moment when he told me, but after Rajesh had left the room, I started freaking out. I was scared and wasn't thinking clearly, and I guess if what happened to my sister ever happened to Rajesh, I didn't want to have to witness that, so, I left, *partially* because I wanted to make sure our relationship problems didn't make him more anxious. I told your father that I was going to leave, and then, well, we argued. I freaked out even more, then left. I knew that your father wouldn't take me back, so I didn't talk to any of you for 7 years. Finally, I found the courage to call your father again. I asked for both your numbers and got yours, Rajesh. He refused to give me yours, Krithi, for some reason. I don't know why. I tried to check in with you to see how you were doing. How did you take that, by the way?"

"Um... fine," Rajesh lied. "Just fine."

"Really?" Mom whispered.

"Yeah," I lied as well.

"Okay, I'm glad. Well, I'm going to go and do something. I'm sorry I couldn't tell the truth sooner," Mom said, and left the room. I stared ahead again and Rajesh stared at the floor. I finally got up and left the room. I walked into one of the many gardens. I couldn't believe how things escalated today. I sat down on a bench, studying a waterfall. I knew my brother and I made a mistake by lying to our mother, but we couldn't tell her the truth and hurt her. I felt a small tear run down my cheek and before I knew it, I was crying silently.

Thirteen

"Krithi!" I heard a voice say. I ignored it and stared straight ahead again. I continued to look at the waterfall until I heard the sound of crutches and the owner of the voice sat down beside me. I turned to my left and found Ajith. I looked at him in confusion.

"What are you doing here?" I asked.

"Rajesh texted us. Chathura and I immediately came as soon as we found out what happened. That must've been hard for you."

"Hard?!" Chathura's voice came from behind. She walked over and sat beside me on my right. "They were just given the hard truth! That would've brought back terrible memories. Are you okay, Krithi?"

I'm fine," I lied.

"Come on, we know you better than that," Ajith said. "How bad was it?"

"It wasn't bad," I said.

"Really?" Chathura asked.

"Yes," I said.

"You know how we know you're lying?" Ajith asked.

"Tell me," I said.

"You're crying right now." It took me a moment to realize that fresh tears were rolling down my face. I tried to dry my eyes and Ajith put his hand on my shoulder, and Chathura rubbed my back. I was able to dry my eyes and I looked straight ahead again.

"Trust me, I'm okay," I said. "The news was just a little too much."

"Don't lie to yourself," Rajesh said, walking towards us. He knelt down in front of the bench.

"We all know that this was really difficult," he said.

"What about you?" I asked.

"Yes, it was hard. I keep getting flashbacks from the day that she left, and don't say that you aren't getting flashbacks either." And now that he brought it up, the scene around me suddenly changed.

I was somehow back in our old house in Amaravati and I found a 7 year old version of myself, who was sitting down on the couch, just staring straight ahead. Rajesh had run over to me, tears in his eyes, explaining everything. I felt fresh tears roll down my face and-

"KRITHI!" A voice yelled. I turned around but couldn't see anything. Then, I felt someone shake me.

"KRITHI!" Someone yelled. Suddenly, I was jerked back to reality, but whoever was shaking me continued. I looked over and it was Chathura.

"Stop," I said. "I snapped out of it!"

"It looks like you were having a flashback," Ajith said, and Chathura stopped shaking me.

"Yeah, I was," I said.

"They'll go away. It's just for the first day," Chathura assured me.

"No offense, but what do you know about flashbacks?" Ajith asked her.

"Um, you're forgetting that our parents dropped me at a boarding school and left me there. It had been 5 years since I saw you again and as soon as I came here, I started having flashbacks about the day I was dropped there."

"Oh, okay. I didn't know," Ajith said. "So why didn't you tell me?"

"You weren't the most understanding brother when we were younger… no offense. I *couldn't* tell you because I was afraid."

"Well, time passed! We were 13 when we met again!"

"Both of you, solve this thing later!" Rajesh suggested. "Why don't we focus on comforting my sister?"

"Right, sorry," Chathura said.

"I'm fine," I lied again.

"What are all of you doing here in this garden?" A voice called from behind. Chathura's eyes widened and Ajith looked irritated. Rajesh looked at them each in confusion, and I did the same, but the voice sounded familiar. I just didn't remember where I had heard it.

"Didn't you hear me? I said-" The voice began again, but Rajesh stopped it mid sentence.

"We heard you," he said. The owner of the voice walked over to the bench.

"I'm assuming something is wrong," she whispered. She kneeled down next to Rajesh and then gasped when she saw Ajith and Chathura.

"Chathura, Ajith…" her voice trailed away. Before she could say anything else, Ajith and Chathura both got up and left the garden quickly. I went after Ajith and Rajesh went after Chathura.

"Hey!" I called after Ajith. Ajith kept heading forward. I put my hand on his shoulder to stop him.

"What happened?" I asked, concerned.

"You don't need to know!" Ajith snapped at me.

"Ajith, I-"

"Go away, Krithi!"

"Just tell me what happened," I said calmly. Ajith glared at me and yelled,

"NO!" I stared at the ground. I knew that Ajith was still glaring at me.

"Why?" I asked, quietly. Ajith sighed. He waited a few seconds then told me,

"It's personal, but I trust you. I can tell you as long as you don't tell anyone else, especially your mother. That person is her friend."

"Who?" I asked.

"Ravima." I never recalled my mother having a friend called Ravima.

"The voice sounded familiar," I said. "I don't remember whose it was, though."

"She lived in Atlantic City. Ring a bell?"

"Yeah." Oh no, now things were coming back to me.

"Oh... that's not just my mother's friend, that's my old therapist."

"Oh my gosh," Ajith whispered.

"It's fine. Just tell me what happened."

"Promise not to think I'm a liar or get angry?"

"I never liked her," I said. "There's no possible way I'll get angry."

"Okay. She is our mother."

"What?!" I gasped.

"Yeah. She lived here in Santa Monica until our father divorced her, and then she moved to Atlantic City and became a therapist," Ajith explained. "Wait a minute. Your depression should've been gone by then!"

"It was. Just in case, when I was 13 years old, my dad made appointments with her."

"Okay, well, she became a therapist in Atlantic City and well... now she moved back here."

"I am so sorry," I said. "That's hard."

"Especially for Chathura. Can you imagine? And... I was acting selfish."

"No, you weren't," I said.

"Yes I was. I was so angry that our mother was here, I didn't even think about how Chathura must've been handling all this."

"Right... the boarding school," I whispered to myself. Ajith stared at me for a couple of seconds.

"I'm sorry I yelled at you," he said quietly, yet sincerely.

"It's okay. I understand," I said. We both headed back to the garden and found Chathura and Rajesh.

"*Don't* tell Krithi, okay?" Chathura said, angrily. Rajesh nodded.

"I already know," I said. "How are you doing, by the way?"

"I'm fine. I don't care and I never will," Chathura snapped.

"Are you sure?" I asked.

"STOP ASKING, KRITHI! YOU DON'T NEED TO KNOW EVERYTHING!" Chathura screamed.

"Stop!" Ajith yelled. He rushed over to a sobbing Chathura and said, "I made the same mistake of yelling at her. It isn't her fault."

"YES IT IS. IT'S NOT JUST HERS, IT'S HER DEMENTED MOTHER'S FAULT! SHE'S THE ONE WHO INVITED *OUR* MOTHER OVER! THEY'RE BOTH AWFUL! AND NOW KRITHI'S PRETENDING TO CARE!"

"Stop yelling at her! This isn't anyone's fault!" Rajesh snapped. "And our mother is *not* demented!" Before I could cry in public again, I ran into the house and into my room. I cried and cried, yet I somehow remained silent the whole time. I felt a hand on my back and I said, "I need to be alone." I assumed it was either my father or Rajesh, or probably even my mother, but when I turned around, I found Ravima.

"Krithi, just keep in mind, Chathura did *not* mean-" I cut her off mid sentence by glaring sharply at her.

"How could you just do that to her?!" I screamed.

"What?"

"Send her over to boarding school! That's awful! Just for one mistake!"

"It's not what you think."

"It looks *clearly* like what I think."

"I didn't send Chathura to that school as a punishment! I sent her... because she needed something we didn't have."

"And what was that?" I snapped.

"Good hospitality. She also needed proper education if she ever wanted to get into any other good school. Ajith was already excelling in many of his subjects! He'd be able to get into other schools easily and we knew that our house in Santa Monica would be better, but Chathura, though? She was barely passing her subjects, just because her teachers were biased. Of course, they stopped teaching altogether, but still. We needed her to actually have good teachers if her academic record was going to be good. We found the school and sent her there, and I knew she'd hate it, but it was for her own good. We did threaten her, though, and that was our fault."

"Oh my gosh," I said.

"Yeah. It was wrong, I know."

"Chathura said you didn't care about how bad the boarding school was."

"I seemed like I didn't. I was in a bad mood that day. I did care, but after that, Chathura refused to listen to me about it. The whole family did, and I don't blame them. Besides, their father and I were not having a good relationship. So, we divorced each other. Chathura and Ajith never really understood the truth, because it's complicated."

"Oh gosh," I murmured.

"I'll go talk to them." Ravima left the room and I sighed. I had no idea about the truth, and now that I knew that Ravima wasn't the parent I thought she was, it made me even more angry about how Chathura burst on me. Fresh tears of anger stung my eyes, and I started crying again. I usually don't get super emotional whenever someone yells at me or takes out their anger on me, but I couldn't really help it this time. Thankfully, I was able to stop soon. A few minutes later, I heard a knock on the door.

"Come in," I muttered. Rajesh came inside.

"What?" I asked.

"Well, Chathura and Ajith... Ravima spoke to them."

"Yeah, what happened?" I asked.

"Um... come to the garden," Rajesh said. We both hurried there, and found Chathura tearing out flowers.

"Hey! *What are you doing*?!" I yelled.

"Taking out my anger on this stupid garden!" Chathura screamed back.

"STOP!" I screamed. I sighed. So much has happened today! I couldn't take it anymore!

"Are you mad?!" I asked. She ignored me.

"Ugh! I can't believe I was so foolish!" Chathura yelled, tearing out another flower.

"Foolish?" I wasn't expecting to hear that.

"Yes! I was so foolish in believing my mother was who I thought she was!" It took me a couple of moments to realize this and then I sighed.

"It's okay. You didn't know what happened," I said.

"I guess so. Krithi, I'm so sorry about the way I blew up on you. And... for what I did to your garden."

"It's alright. There isn't much damage," I said, looking around. She only tore out a few flowers and it was barely visible. I smiled calmly. "And I know you were angry," I added.

"Today's been a long day," Rajesh sighed.

"I agree," I said.

"Um... we should probably go," Ajith said.

"Yeah," Chathura agreed. They immediately left, and Rajesh and I went back to our rooms. We didn't do much that day, and we focused on our own things. After all of that drama, we couldn't take anything else.

Fourteen

The weekend ended quickly, and I was glad about it. We headed back to school, went through our classes, and my friends, my brother, and I practically avoided each other the whole day. Classes went by quickly and I had acrobatics today.

"Krithi, hi! So... good news. Ajith will be recovered by the time of Nationals. You can use the week before the competition to practice with him. For now, though, practice your original routine. You haven't been registered yet. We'll register you on the last week."

"Okay," I said. I attempted a double twist and failed, like usual.

"Try a front full," Chenglei suggested. "You've been giving up on everything else. This is a slightly easier move."

"I've been trying!" I snapped back. "I've been falling over and over again!"

"Are you trying to get a perfect score or not?!" Chenglei asked. I sighed.

"I am," I said, quietly. I continued practicing other moves and a lot of time must've passed, because Mrs. Sayuri said,

"Class is over. See you at the next class." I immediately ran out of there, changed back into regular clothes, and headed to the food court, to find Ajith waiting there alone.

"Hey," I said.

"Oh, hi," he said. He walked away and I walked the other direction. I ordered something and walked over to a table. I sat alone and ate quietly.

Afterwards, I headed over to the Asia Wing common room and sat there by myself, not doing anything. Ajith, Rajesh and Chathura soon showed up and walked over to me.

"Hi."

"What's up?" Chathura said.

"Nothing," I said.

"Okay, look, we've all been avoiding each other today. Why?" Rajesh said.

"You know why!" I said.

"Okay, well, can we stop avoiding each other?" Chathura suggested. "It's driving me crazy. Okay? It's one time where things went wrong. We can't just avoid each other forever!"

"Fine," I said.

"Good. Now change of topic. The dance is on Friday!" Chathura said.

"Oh my gosh, seriously?!" Rajesh muttered.

"What, you forgot to go tuxedo shopping?" Chathura smirked. Rajesh glared at her.

"I told you, I already *have* one. Anyways, that's not why, it's just... it seems a little soon, don't you think?"

"Not really. Anyways, Krithi, are you going to go to the dance?"

"Sure," I said. "I'll go."

"Ajith will you be able to?" Chathura asked.

"I'm definitely not. I found out from a doctor earlier today that my ankle will take up to 6 weeks to heal. Since the sprain was minor, it'll probably take 4 or 5 weeks," Ajith said.

"Okay," I said. "Oh, and speaking of which, Mrs. Sayuri said that you can compete in the National competition, but just in case, she told me to practice my routine with Chenglei."

"Alright then."

"Wait, Krithi, are you going with anyone?" Chathura asked, eyeing Chenglei.

"If you're hinting that I should go with Chenglei, then no. Just no."

"Oh come on! I mean, I get that he's annoying and all, but still! At least you'll have a date!"

"I'd rather go without a date," I said.

"You'll be fine," Chathura persuaded me.

"Why do you want me to do this?" I asked.

"Oh my gosh," Ajith muttered quietly to himself, placing his hand on his forehead, anxiously.

"Oh, I'm just lightly suggesting," Chathura said, sheepishly.

"Chathura, there's clearly some other reason!" Rajesh said. "You can't *just* be suggesting my sister goes to the dance with someone she hates."

"Well..." Chathura said quietly.

"If you don't tell her, I will," Ajith snapped.

"Tell me *what*?!" I asked. Chathura looked down at the ground guiltily.

"Fine. Chenglei signed up to perform an acrobatics routine for the dance, and he needs a partner, so I told him you'd do it."

"WHAT?!" I yelled.

"I'm sorry, Krithi! Chenglei was begging for you to be his-" I held my hand up to stop her.

"I'll do it," I muttered flatly. I walked over to Chenglei.

"I'll be your partner for the acrobatics routine, but this is the *only* time we are dancing together," I said quickly. "Besides the acrobatics competition," I added when he raised his eyebrows.

"I told you we would date one day," Chenglei said, triumphantly.

"We are *not* dating!" I snapped, and walked away. I went back to my friends, and Chathura looked at me nervously.

"How did it go?" Rajesh asked.

"Bad," I said.

"So, when are you going to plan your routine?"

"I don't know."

"Knowing Chenglei, he'd probably want to create a routine on the spot," Chathura said.

"What?!" I gasped. "That never goes well."

"That might be your only option... sorry," Chathura said quietly.

"Ugh, whatever happened to getting a perfect score?!"

"You'll be fine," Ajith said.

"Fine, I trust you. I mean, you score high whenever you do that, don't you?" I told him.

"It was only one routine that I created spontaneously, because it never really needed planning. The rest of them I planned. Anyways, this isn't exactly an acrobatics competition, you're just performing, so I feel like it should be okay for you to do it spontaneously... just this one time."

"Okay."

"Change of topic, Krithi, when are you going to get a dress for the dance?" Chathura asked.

"I already have one," I answered. "I packed it just in case I was going."

"Oh, I can't wait to see it!" Chathura gushed.

"You'll see on Friday," I said.

"I'm sure it's amazing," Ajith said. Chathura gave him a smirk, and he rolled his eyes.

"What? It's just a friendly compliment," Ajith muttered, blushing slightly.

"Mhm... *sure* it is," Chathura teased, earning herself a glare from Rajesh. "And do you blush every time you give a friendly compliment?"

"What?!" Ajith snapped. "I didn't blush!" I laughed a little.

"Thank you," I said, redirecting their conversation. Ajith smiled at me, and I returned it.

"We should go to bed now," I suggested after a couple seconds. The others nodded, and we headed back to our dormitories for some sleep.

I was so busy that I hadn't even realized that many days had passed and soon enough, it was the day of the dance. I was in my dormitory, getting ready. I decided to wear a rose gold sheath dress, and I also wore some black flats, some lip gloss, a little blush, and some eyeliner. For a hairstyle, I did a half up braid, since I rarely do that and it was a special occasion.

Chathura walked inside and I turned around.

"Oh my gosh. You look beautiful!" Chathura gushed.

"Thank you. So do you!" I said, smiling and studying Chathura's outfit, which was a pink overskirt dress, flats, and a little bit of pink eyeshadow and pink lip gloss.

"Thanks! Now, let's go!" Chathura said. We walked out of our dormitory and met Rajesh in a hallway. He was wearing a blue tuxedo that our mother had got him from India. Chathura bumped into him and gasped.

"Oh, sorry!"

"It's fine," Rajesh replied. "You look beautiful. Krithi, you look really nice too."

"Thanks," I said, smiling.

"Let's go," Chathura said. We all headed to the auditorium, and we found multiple people dancing.

"Krithi!" A voice called. "Ready?"

"For?" I asked, turning around and finding Chenglei.

"The acrobatics routine?"

"Well, we didn't really plan anything, so... not really," I said. Chenglei sighed and said,

"We're making up everything on the spot, okay? I'm not taking no for an answer."

"Whatever." Clearly, Chenglei knew nothing about organization.

"And now, Krithi Sridhar and Chenglei Tao will perform an acrobatics routine for your entertainment," Mr. Chang announced. I gasped and turned around, glaring at Chenglei.

"NOW?!" I screamed.

"Yes, now!" Chenglei yelled back. "I told Mr. Chang we'd do it at the beginning of the school dance… and now I'm realizing I *didn't* tell you." Chathura widened her eyes in shock, and Rajesh glared at Chenglei.

"Oh my gosh, I cannot believe you!" I snapped as I shook my head in disbelief. We walked on the stage and Chenglei whispered,

"Get into a position!" Apparently, my "position" was leaning on him. "What are you doing?" I whispered to him. He immediately spun away, and I nearly fell on the ground. Thankfully, I got into a back handspring and landed it. I went into two side aerials, and did a back tuck. We continued doing a bunch of tumbling moves and other movements, and we finally (and thankfully) finished the so-called acrobatics routine. People applauded and I went off the stage quickly.

"That was awful," I muttered to myself.

"Krithi, I recorded the routine so that I could send it to you, and you have to look at this!" Chathura gasped. She showed me her phone. I widened my eyes in shock. The whole time I was doing the routine, Chenglei was doing something else. Something that was so graceful and amazing, that I looked like a fool on stage. It wasn't even a properly assembled acrobatics routine! It looked like everything was in pieces. I covered my eyes with my hands. That had to be the most embarrassing moment of my life!

"What happened?" Rajesh asked.

"This," Chathura said, showing him her phone.

"Oh my gosh," Rajesh gasped. "Krithi, I am so sorry."

"It's fine," I lied. Chenglei was *still* on stage, and people continued cheering. Then, people started saying things like,

"Do it without the girl next time!"

"Yeah, the girl is a fool!" I fought back tears of anger and humiliation and I glared at Chenglei who *finally* went off stage.

"Good job," he said.

"What do you mean 'good job'?!" Rajesh snapped. "You purposely tried to make her look bad! And don't deny it!"

"Didn't you listen to what everyone was saying about her?" Chathura asked.

"Who said I was trying to make her look bad?" Chenglei asked. I stared at him and said,

"You didn't have to say anything. It was obvious." I turned away and began to walk out of the auditorium.

"Krithi, wait!" Chathura called, but I ignored her as I ran out of the auditorium as quickly as I could (thank goodness I was just wearing flats), and continued running until I ran into someone. I gasped in fear as I stumbled and whoever I ran into caught me. They helped me back into a stable position, and I looked up and saw Ajith. I turned red in embarrassment and horror. He simply stood on one leg, grabbed his crutches from the side of the wall and stabilized himself.

"Sorry!" I said.

"Are you okay? You were bolting as if something terrible happened," he said. "What happened?"

"Chenglei," I muttered. I didn't have to say anything else. Ajith was able to make the connection.

"Something happened during the routine, didn't it?"

"Yes. I don't know if I should even be talking about it," I said.

"I'll listen to you if you want to tell me," he said.

"Fine. No one's in the Asia Wing common room. I'll tell you there." We headed to the Asia Wing common room and sat down somewhere. I slowly explained everything, and Ajith remained calm.

"I'll talk to him," he said.

"No! Don't do that!" I said.

"Why? He won't listen to anyone who's angry with him, like my sister, or your brother. He might listen to me, though, because I am a bit calmer."

"That makes sense," I said.

"I'll speak to him another time," he said. "I can't really be in the auditorium, can I?" I soon heard footsteps, and when I looked, Rajesh, Hui Ying, and Chathura were all heading over to us.

"Hi," I said.

"Are you okay?" Chathura asked.

"I'm fine," I lied, trying to keep my patience.

"Are you though?" Ajith asked me. I looked at the ground and didn't say anything.

"It's okay to tell the truth," Hui Ying said. I glared at them all, and the one ounce of patience I had suddenly went away.

"I'm fine, okay?!" I snapped and I immediately left the common room and headed towards my dormitory. I went over to my bed and tried meditating on my feelings (my mother taught me this technique). I continued until I heard footsteps. I turned off the app I was using quickly and walked out of my dormitory.

"Krithi!!" Chathura screamed as I accidentally ran into her. She looked scared.

"What happened?!" I asked.

"Rajesh," she said, fear reflecting in her eyes. I gasped and ran over to the Asia Wing common room and found Rajesh crying uncontrollably... *again*.

Fifteen

"What happened this time?!" I asked. No one said anything. I threw them a sharp glare.

"I said, *what happened this time*?!" I screamed. Finally, Hui Ying looked at me.

"Um... you may get a little scared," she said. "Try your best to remain calm."

"What happened?!" I asked for the third time.

"Your mother had a dizzy spell and passed out," Ajith said, as he walked towards me. "She's in the hospital right now. They're trying to figure out what's going on." I covered my mouth in shock. Tears rolled down my cheek as Ajith wrapped his arm around my shoulders.

"Rajesh... someone needs to help him-" I began, but Ajith cut me off mid sentence.

"Chathura's on it."

"I need to see my mother," I said, and now I was the one crying uncontrollably. I tried to stop but as I wiped my eyes, more tears started spilling out.

"Shh," Ajith whispered. "You'll see her tomorrow. Chathura was able to call your father."

"Thank you," I said. It had been 5 minutes until I found Rajesh by my side.

"Are you okay?" I asked him.

"Yes, I'm good. Are you?" I shook my head, for once admitting the truth about how I really felt.

"It's okay," he said. "We'll see her. It's probably nothing." I hoped it was nothing. I immediately left the common room again and headed back to my dormitory, trying to stop thinking about it. It was impossible, and I couldn't necessarily blame myself.

The next day, our father took us both to the hospital to see our mother. As soon as we reached the hospital, we immediately went into her room.

"Mom," Rajesh whispered.

"Hi," she whispered back.

"Are you okay?" I asked.

"Yes, I'm fine. Don't worry. According to the doctor, I was probably extremely dehydrated."

"Thank goodness," I said.

"Don't worry. I'll be fine soon."

"Unfortunately, it's not just dehydration," a voice said. I turned around and found a doctor rushing towards my mother. Dad gasped and so did we.

"We ran tests. She's got anemia... and other possible conditions. We will keep her here for some time to monitor her, since her case is a little unusual. We're trying to figure out what else happened."

"Oh my gosh," I whispered.

"I'll be okay. I want you all to focus on your own things, okay? Krithi, focus on your acrobatics competition. It's in 5 weeks. Rajesh, focus on what you like doing, okay?" Mom said.

"Alright," I said, a little uneasy about it. We left the room and immediately headed home. I immediately went upstairs into my room. A few minutes later, Rajesh came inside.

"Hey," I said.

"Hey," he replied. "Can I tell you something?"

"Go ahead," I said.

"I... knew that something was going on with Mom. I've known since the competition in San Jose. She said not to tell you, because you have a lot on your plate right now."

"What?" I gasped.

"I'm so sorry," Rajesh sighed. "It's all my fault."

"Hey, don't blame yourself," I said, taking his hand. "You didn't know what to do."

"Thank you," Rajesh said, smiling timidly.

"Both of you," Dad said, walking inside. "I know you are scared, but please do not worry."

"How can we not?" Rajesh asked.

"Please. Your mother doesn't want you to worry. Trust me, everything will be okay," Dad assured us.

"Fine, we will try," I agreed.

"Thank you."

The weekend went by quickly again, and we found ourselves back at the ISI, trying to forget everything.

"Hey!" A voice yelled. I turned around and found Mr. Chang behind me.

"Um..."

"I'm not scolding you, if that's what you think. Your father told me that your biological mother is hospitalized, and that you might not be able to focus in class. Just, you and your brother, take it easy."

"Thanks, but I'm fine," I said. "And so is Rajesh."

"Okay, just let us know if you need a break from anything," he said.

"Fine," I said. I walked over to my elective class and today we were studying performing arts. He gave us an assignment and once the class was over, I headed over to my math class, where I ran into Ajith.

"Hi," I said.

"Hey. I heard what happened, are you okay?"

"I'm fine, we should head over to math," I said. We both walked over to the classroom and took our seats.

"Class," our teacher said. "We will be having a pop test on linear functions." It was at that moment when I found out that I had forgotten to study for the test. Thankfully, I knew linear functions by heart and could hopefully get a good grade on it. I took out my pencil and started filling out the test in front of me. As soon as I was finished, I handed my test to our teacher, and she whispered,

"You know, you didn't have to take this test today if you were deal-"

"Thanks, but I'm fine," I stopped her mid sentence and walked back to my desk. Soon, all classes were over, and I made my way over to acrobatics.

"Hi, Krithi!" Mrs. Sayuri said. "Just so you know, if it's too much with everything going on-"

"I am fine," I said. I walked over to an open space and began practicing.

"Hey," Chenglei said.

"What do you want?" I asked rudely, not looking at him.

"I wanted to tell you that I wasn't trying to make you look bad that day at the dance," he said.

"Oh yeah... you weren't trying to make me look bad. *You were trying to make me look awful*!"

"Why would I do that?!" Chenglei asked.

"You were rude to me the first day we met, and after that, you pretended to have a crush on me, and I kept rejecting you, so you decided to get revenge on me by humiliating me in front of the whole school... or at least in front of everyone who attended that stupid dance. Thanks to you, I was a laughing stock there!"

"Okay, just because I accidentally made you look bad, doesn't mean you can yell at me this way! You're just a drama queen, freaking out for the smallest things!" I whirled around and glared at him.

"Oh yeah?" I asked. "You have no idea what's been going on! My life was never a perfect 10, unlike yours, okay?!"

"And that's all *my* fault?!"

"No," I admitted after waiting a couple of seconds. "But don't call me a drama queen, okay? I am not freaking out just because of you." Chenglei sighed.

"To make it up to you, I can help you with something."

"I don't want your help," I snapped. Acrobatics thankfully ended at that moment. I changed back into my uniform in a changing room next to the studio and I ran into Hui Ying outside.

"I just saw what happened," she said before I could say anything. "And Ajith did as well. And Chathura."

"Oh my gosh," I muttered under my breath.

"It's okay. We get it, Chenglei can be really annoying, and given everything you're going through at the moment, it's understandable why you got so upset with him, but I think that it's been easier for you to blame all of your emotions on one person rather than face them on your own. I can understand why, but it's not the best idea to do that, because you can end up hurting your friends and family, and even the people you don't exactly get along with well," Ajith told me. "Don't you remember what happened with Rajesh?"

"How can I forget?" I asked. "Even now I feel like he's still mad at me. Anyways, I get what you mean."

"Good," he said.

"There's something else we need to talk about," Chathura said.

"What is it?" I asked.

"You're hiding your emotions and trying to show a different version of yourself. We all know that you're upset about what happened to your mother. She's someone you care about! It's hard when these things happen, and you don't have to fake it in front of everyone. I talked to Rajesh, and he told me how he really felt."

"Really?" I asked.

"Yeah. You're usually the only one he'll talk about his emotions with, but this was way too much for him."

"I know," I said. "It's... been a lot for me too, but I really just don't want to talk about it to every teacher who asks me about it, so I say I'm fine. You three and Rajesh are the only people I can actually talk to about my feelings, and even that's hard."

"I feel like you've been hiding your true self in front of us," Hui Ying admitted. "Have you been faking your true self since the day we met? Oh, and please answer me honestly. All I'm trying to do is help." It took almost all of my restraint not to get mad at her for asking.

"Um... it's not really like I've been faking my true self. I am my current true self in front of you, but let's just say I'm not the same person I was back when I was living in India."

"Really? What changed that?" Chathura asked.

"You know what changed that!" I snapped.

"Sometimes admitting these things out loud can help you find your solution. That at least works for me, but I'm not sure about you," Chathura explained.

"Okay, fine. My mother left us."

"And did you talk to her?"

"You know very well-" I began but stopped. Chathura was raising her eyebrows and I thought about what she said about admitting these things out loud. I sighed.

"Yes, I did," I said.

"Exactly. She told you the reason she left, and I know it was hard, but don't you think she wasn't even sure of what her mistake was?"

"True."

"And now that she's here in Santa Monica, she's seeing you more often. She realized her mistake, and she really cares about you."

"I know," I said. "I was really glad things were going back to normal, and then I found out that she has anemia... and possibly other bad conditions, she passed out, and now she's under close supervision at the hospital." I held back tears, but it was really hard. I didn't want to cry.

"Hey," Ajith said, rubbing my shoulder. "She'll be just fine after she gets her blood transfusion done, okay? Don't worry."

"Yeah," Chathura added. "We'll always listen to you if you are comfortable expressing your emotions." I felt a huge surge of gratitude and I smiled softly.

"Thank you so much. You three have been so amazing since I came here. I don't know what I'd do without you," I told them. They responded with a smile, and we made our way over to the food court and found Rajesh, who looked worried.

"Hey. I have bad news," he said.

"What happened? Is it about Mom?!" I started to panic. Rajesh quickly grabbed my shoulder to stop me from freaking out.

"No, no, she's okay," he assured me. "It's about your acrobatics competition."

"What?" I asked.

"They've moved the date of it. It's this Saturday."

Sixteen

"WHAT?!" I exclaimed. "It wasn't supposed to be for another 4 or 5 weeks!"

"I know, but to adjust to everyone's preferences, they had to change it."

"Oh my gosh," I muttered.

"It's okay," Hui Ying said. "You already practiced your routine! You'll be okay."

"Okay," I said. "Thanks for reminding me."

"I'm so sorry," Rajesh said.

"Not your fault," I replied, leaving my friends and finding a table to sit by myself.

"Does she always cool down by being alone?" I overheard Hui Ying ask.

"Yes," Rajesh replied to her. I rolled my eyes as I ordered something and ate by myself. After that, I headed straight to my dormitory. I then opened the fountain pen and ink cartridges that my mother gave me and stuck a pink one inside the pen. Pink is my mother's favorite color, so I decided to use it to make a card for her. I also packed an art set when I came here, so I opened that and used the materials in that to work on the card. I began making the card, and I was working for so long, I didn't even realize that Hui Ying and Chathura entered the room. As soon as I finished, I put it in an envelope and laid it on my desk. I looked at them and smiled. They smiled back. I went into my bed and slept peacefully, without worrying for once.

The next day, acrobatics was a little chaotic. I practiced a routine with Chenglei, until I overheard a scream. Araceli and Alan managed to get into an argument. Everyone was just staring at it, and I figured that I needed to take action. This was supposed to stop, and quickly too!

"Okay, both of you, STOP,"Mrs. Sayuri yelled (thankfully).

"This doesn't concern you!" Araceli said. I looked at her in shock.

"You'd better watch it, Araceli. You're forgetting that even though I am an extracurricular coach, I can *still* land you in detention," Mrs. Sayuri reprimanded her. "And for your information, this *does* concern me, because it's happening here in *my* gymnasium!"

"I'm glad she tried to stop us. Why don't you tell her, Araceli? Everything you did to me. You trash talked my sister, then you posted a video of me online! And I'm *just* getting started," Alan growled. Mrs. Sayuri gave up and stared at me, and so did the rest of the team. I rolled my eyes. It looks like now *I* had to stop it. I sighed.

"Araceli, explain what happened."

"Well, I never did anything to Alan. Someone framed me for all of this. I wouldn't do that to him."

"Okay. Alan, explain," I said.

"There's no way Araceli would do what she did. I know her better than that, but her personality has been changing so much recently, that I can't help but believe that she was actually the one to do that."

"I wasn't!" Araceli said. "I'm really not the person who I show on the outside. I've tried to hide my true self for a long time now."

"Really?" Alan asked. "Why?" Araceli sighed and said flatly,

"I lived in Spain, moved to Mexico, then moved here. Within that time frame, horrible things happened, and I don't want to talk about them."

"That's okay," Alan said. "I'm sorry for believing that you were the one to do all of this. I wonder who framed you, though."

"I don't know. It's best to leave all of that behind us, though," Araceli said.

"Totally," Alan said. I smiled. I was relieved that the whole argument was over. I went back to practicing my routine with Chenglei, and Mrs. Sayuri walked over to me.

"Hey, by the way, thank you for stopping their argument. It's been so intense these past few weeks with those two. Oh, and I love what you're doing. Just take this as a suggestion. I suggest you add the throw and catch to your dynamic routine. It'll give you extra points."

"You know I can't do it," I said.

"It's okay. Just take it as a suggestion."

"Alright," I agreed. I practiced a few extra moves. I tried it out with Chenglei and still fell.

"Try using more power. Not too much, though," Chenglei said.

"I am never taking advice from you," I snapped. He stalked away and I continued practicing by myself. As soon as acrobatics was over, I changed into my uniform, and met Rajesh in the food court.

"Where are the others?" I asked.

"They'll be here soon. Also, Mr. Chang said we can meet our mother on Thursday."

"Oh, that's great!" I said. All of my nervous feelings soon went away as I spent some time with my friends. I was glad of it, and was able to be unafraid for once.

The next day went by quickly, and then Dad picked us up again, and we headed to the hospital. He seemed worried, so I asked, "What's going on?"
"Nothing."
"Dad, it's obvious you're hiding something," Rajesh said.
"Fine. You'll see at the hospital." We arrived and found my mother unconscious next to way more advanced equipment.
"What happened?!" I gasped.
"She's had a seizure," the doctor explained. "She'll be alright, though. Unfortunately, we need her to go to another doctor for her treatment. It is overly expensive, though, and unfortunately we can't help her case, which we aren't even able to determine. The best we could do is put her in a coma."
"Oh my gosh," Rajesh whispered. I covered my mouth in horror. Christina was apparently on some business trip where her phone didn't have any messaging service except for one texting platform that none of us had, so it wasn't possible for us to talk to her about this. We had to somehow get the money ourselves. I placed the envelope that contained the card I made next to her on the bedside table, and we immediately left the hospital, and Dad dropped us off at the ISI. We walked inside, and found our friends at the Asia Wing common room.

"Hey, how is your mother?" Ajith asked. I shook my head and started crying. I seriously wanted to stop, but I couldn't.

"It got worse, didn't it?" He said. I nodded.

"She had a seizure," Rajesh told him. "She was put in a coma, and that was unfortunately the best option."

"Oh my gosh. Is she going to be okay?" Ajith asked and I glared at him.

"What do you think?!" I asked, drying my eyes.

"I was just asking," Ajith answered, quietly. He remained silent after.

"Krithi, *please* don't get angry with him. He's trying to help you," Rajesh told me.

"He is asking questions that have an obvious answer! You know I hate that!" I yelled.

"Krithi, calm down. We have a solution," Hui Ying said.

"What?" I asked, desperately.

"Rajesh told me everything. The new doctor is really expensive, right? Well, whoever wins Nationals wins a cash prize of 2,000 dollars. You've got a chance."

"Rajesh, you've seriously told her about the price?!" I snapped.

"I didn't tell her anything-" Rajesh tried to tell me calmly, but I stopped him mid sentence.

"Then how does she know?!"

"Stop!" Chathura yelled to break the argument. "We made a guess, because there is one specific hospital that does the best treatment for patients. Anyways, you have to do what Mrs. Sayuri said. Add the throw and catch to your routine."

"I can't," I said.

"Then, try to do everything perfectly. Those are your only two solutions. I'm sorry, but there is nothing else you can do."

"Okay," I agreed. I wasn't ready, but it was worth a try.

Seventeen

The next evening, we flew to Dallas. Ajith, Chathura, Hui Ying, and Rajesh decided to come as well to support me. I couldn't imagine how they would ever do such a thing after the way I acted yesterday, but I was glad that they decided to. They were allowed to, as long as they headed back to the school before Tuesday (we had Monday off). We boarded the plane and landed in about three hours. We immediately went to our hotel and I was assigned a room with Mrs. Sayuri, Vanessa, and Ajith again. I refused to speak to both of them because I wasn't in the mood to, and I was scared of what Ajith would say to me if I even did speak to him. We slept immediately so that we'd be ready for tomorrow, though I wasn't sure if I would be.

The next day, we checked in for the competition and I warmed up alone (I usually warm up with Vanessa or Ajith). Soon enough, I met my father and Rajesh who both wished me good luck.

"All the best," Rajesh said to me.

"Thanks," I said, quietly. He smiled.

"Hey, can I talk to you for a second?" I asked.

"Sure," he said. We walked to an area where there weren't many people.

"I'm so sorry about the way I've been acting lately. I know there's no excuse for it, and I've done so many awful things-" Rajesh stopped me mid sentence by taking my hand.

"It's okay," he told me.

"What?"

"It's fine. Everyone makes mistakes from time to time. It's a good thing that you realized it, and you're fixing it by speaking to me right now. And... I completely understand why you were acting the way you were. We were both going through so much." I was extremely glad that he was able to get over it that easily and understand. I am so grateful to have someone like him.

"Thank you," I said.

"No problem. Now, I think they want you somewhere." I smiled at him and headed to the area where I was supposed to wait. Sienna and Alan were dancing first. I watched them until I felt a hand on my shoulder. I turned around.

"Ajith!" I gasped.

"Hi," he replied back.

"They let you backstage?"

"I'm technically still on the team," he pointed out. "Even if I've got a sprained ankle and can't compete."

"Right," I said. "Look, I am so sorry about the way I've been acting. I've been so awful lately and I have no idea how to make it up to you, but if I can in any way, just let me know."

"It's totally alright, you don't have to. I get how you were feeling. I just want you to know though, I wasn't trying to aggravate you or anything by asking. I was actually not sure if your mother was going to be alright or anything... and it's also a natural question that comes to everyone's mind."

"I know, I'm sorry I got so mad at you. I'm not even sure how she's doing," I said.

"She'll be okay. My mom said that Aishwarya is a strong woman, and I know I'm, like, the third or fourth person to suggest this, but please add the throw and catch to your routine."

"Isn't it too late?" I asked.

"You can still do it if you try. Chenglei has been encouraging you since you both have practiced together," Ajith said. I raised my eyebrows.

"You want me to trust *Chenglei*?" I asked skeptically.

"Maybe it's about time that you did. He has been trying to apologize to you for the events that happened during the school dance for a while now." I smiled, but it soon turned into a worried expression.

"I'm just too scared," I admitted.

"Try to face your fear," Ajith said. I shrugged. Soon, my name and Chenglei's were announced and I went stiff.

"You can do it," Ajith encouraged me. I walked on stage and smiled nervously at the judges. They signaled that we should do our routines, and so we began them. We successfully finished two of three routines. When it was finally time for the most difficult routine, I remembered what Chenglei said about the power in the throw and catch and what Hui Ying told me about the cash prize. To start the throw and catch, I had to stand on Chenglei's hands, which was scary, because his hands were trembling a bit. I took a deep breath, jumped, and did a full twist upside down in the air. I pleaded with myself to land it, and soon I heard a huge surge of applause. I soon realized that I landed it the correct way. I let out a huge sigh of relief and went off stage knowing I had finally faced my fears.

"Krithi, wow! That was amazing!" Ajith congratulated me. I smiled.

"Thank you!" I said.

"Krithi, thanks to you, ISI has a shot at winning!" Araceli said. I nodded. The judges went on stage and began to speak.

"Everyone who came to this competition did a wonderful job. Now, to announce the winners of this year's competition, individual and team." I crossed my fingers.

"The team winner of this year's National competition is the International School of Immigrants!" The whole team began to scream and congratulate each other, but Ajith and I didn't, as usual. Instead, I continued staring at the judges.

"The individual pair winner for the 14 year old dancers had done such a performance, that our decision was bound to be this one. They took a huge risk in their routine today and it really paid off! The individual winner of this year's National competition is..." I breathed deeply. Ajith took my hand and smiled reassuringly. I knew I had landed a good move, but I didn't know if I messed up on any of the other moves. Suddenly, I heard screaming and applause and I knew they announced who won, but I didn't hear it, because I was so lost in thought.

"Krithi!" Vanessa shook me. "You and Chenglei won the individual competition!"

"What?!" I gasped. I covered my mouth in shock. The rest of the team started congratulating me, and pushed me back onto the stage for the medaling process. Chenglei and I were presented the 1st place medals and the cash prize.

"Krithi, take it," he said after we left the stage. He handed me the prize, but I didn't take it.

"That isn't fair," I said. "We need to split it. It's the only way that would be fair."

"You need that for your mother," Chenglei insisted. I stared at him in shock. How did he know? I don't recall telling him!

"I can tell that you're curious as to *how* I know that," he said, laughing.

"Um..."

"Hui Ying is my cousin. *Don't* get mad at her, I talked her into telling me."

"Okay," I shrugged, still a little shocked at the news.

"Well, anyways, I think you should keep this," Chenglei continued. "For your mother." I smiled and said,

"No, I'm sure 1,000 would be enough."

"If you insist." We split everything equally and I smiled.

"Thank you for your support. If it weren't for you, I wouldn't have been able to do it at all."

"No problem. Sorry I gave you such a hard time since the day we met. I promise though, that night at the dance. That was accidental," Chenglei said.

"I believe you now. Sorry for not listening to you," I told him. He smiled and we both headed to meet our parents, but I stopped in my tracks as soon as I felt a sharp hand grab my shoulder. I whirled around quickly.

"Mrs. Félicité?" I asked. I wasn't shocked about this. There was no way her team *didn't* make it to Nationals.

"Look, I don't know how Hiroko managed to get you all to Nationals in the first place, since her team is filled with such terrible dancers, but... that move you pulled off with that Asian boy was *incredible.*"

"Sorry?" I said, believing I misheard her. She let out a huge, dramatic sigh before saying,

"I said, that move you pulled off with the Asian boy was incredible. I mean it."

"Really?" I gasped. I couldn't believe Mrs. Félicité was *actually* praising me.

"I do." She smiled, this time, a sincere and kind one, though she quickly shook her head and her stern expression covered her face once again.

"But *don't* think that you can stop us next time!" She stalked away and I shook my head, smiling a little. I walked away and ran over to my father and brother..

"Krithi, I've never seen you do such an advanced move!" Dad gushed.

"I can't believe you landed that! You conquered your fears," Rajesh said. I smiled at him.

"I had to face my fears at one point," I said, smiling. Everyone continued congratulating each other, and for once, I wasn't overwhelmed.

Things turned out wonderful after that. Chenglei and I finally started becoming friends and we occasionally helped each other with different acrobatic skills. I was able to give 1,000 dollars to the new hospital to help with the payment for my mother's treatment, which really helped (she was transferred to the new hospital for better care and treatment). I aced pretty much every academic subject in the school, and even got into a few Honors classes! I also managed to do even more advanced moves in acrobatics, getting ready for Worlds. Worlds was a few months away, and would probably be the hardest thing I ever do, but I knew that I was ready for whatever was coming next.

Acknowledgements

Writing this book was one of my favorite things to do during my free time. It was definitely hard, but it was quite fun and a great learning experience (this is my first realistic fiction book), and I wouldn't have ever been able to complete writing this book if it weren't for my friends, family, and everyone else who helped me throughout this journey. I am so glad that I had them there to help.

The first person I would like to thank is my 7th grade History and ELA teacher, Ms. Bjorkquist. In ELA, we would write narratives often, and we actually all wrote a short realistic fiction draft. After reading mine over, she gave me great advice to improve in case I write another realistic fiction story, which in this case, I did write another one, and her advice was very helpful. Thank you, Ms. Bjorkquist.

I would like to thank my best friend Suhani for reviewing this book. She would also always listen to me if I were to ever talk about ideas for characters or if I talked about the plot of the book. Your advice was great and it really made the book better. Thank you, Suhani.

Thanks to my parents and my uncle for reviewing this book as well. Your advice and feedback are very valuable to me, and I couldn't have created a successful book without you. Thanks again to all three of you.

I'd like to give a special thanks to my mom and dad for listening to me anytime I'd talk to them about this book! They were always glad whenever I read a small part to them. Thank you both!

I'd like to thank my mom for helping me come up with the idea for the design for the book cover, and my friend Ishan for creating the cover based on the idea. The cover looks fantastic and really reflects the idea of the story. Thank you again!

I would like to thank my friend Tanvi Ambekar (one of the authors of The Home of Unfortunates series) for giving me advice on this book. Anytime I told you about a scene or had you read over one, you would gladly do so and give me advice that really made the scenes better or give me ideas for new ones. Thank you so much!

I'd like to say thank you to everyone who helped me throughout this journey. You are all so amazing and I couldn't have done it without you.

About The Author

Twisha Rao is 13 years old. She is very passionate about writing and singing and loves to act and participate in musicals. Her favorite and best school subjects are Mathematics and English, and she loves school in general. She started writing at the age of 9, when she was in 3rd grade, just for herself, and started trying to write for an audience when she was 11 years old, in 5th grade. At the age of 12, when she was in 7th grade, she successfully published her first book, and she began to write Perfect 10 a couple months afterwards. This year, Twisha is in 8th grade, and will be spending time writing her other series (The Glass Crystal Prism), and possibly other novels.